THE GOLDEN AQUARIANS

THE GOLDEN AQUARIANS

MONICA HUGHES

Simon & Schuster Books for Young Readers

 SIMON & SCHUSTER BOOKS FOR YOUNG READERS
An imprint of Simon & Schuster Children's Publishing Division
1230 Avenue of the Americas
New York, New York 10020

Published by arrangement with HarperCollins Publishers Ltd., Toronto, Canada.
SIMON & SCHUSTER BOOKS FOR YOUNG READERS is a trademark of Simon & Schuster.
Book design by Virginia Pope.
The text of this book is set in New Caledonia.
Manufactured in the United States of America
10 9 8 7 6 5 4 3 2 1

Library of Congress Cataloging-in-Publication Data
Hughes, Monica.
The Golden Aquarians / Monica Hughes.
p. cm.
Summary: Walt Elliot goes with the father he hasn't seen for years to the planet Aqua, where he discovers that his father's project threatens the existence of a highly intelligent native species.
ISBN 0-671-50543-2
[1. Fathers and sons—Fiction. 2. Environmental protection—Fiction. 3. Extraterrestrial beings—Fiction. 4. Science fiction.] I. Title.
PZ7.H87364Go 1995 [Fic]—dc20 94-12980

Also by Monica Hughes:

The Crystal Drop
Invitation to the Game
The Promise

THE GOLDEN AQUARIANS

Walt's father made planets. At least, that's what Walt thought his Aunt Gloria meant when she tried to explain, when Walt was six, why his father never came home. He used to imagine him, a bit like God, rolling up pieces of clay into worlds and spinning them out into the galaxy.

When he was older he understood that his father headed a team of scientists and workers who went to horrible and unlivable planets and changed them into places more comfortable for Earth colonists to live in. That was almost as good. Meanwhile his father never came home and Walt went on living with Aunt Gloria in Lethbridge, Alberta.

Aunt Gloria called Walt's father "my brother the colonel," and she was very proud of him, almost as proud as Walt was, though he kind of wished she wouldn't boast about him *every* time they went to pick up groceries or buy an ice-cream cone. She never spoke of her brother as "Angus," and Walt found out his father's first name only when he came across a newspaper clipping with the headline: ALBERTA ASTRONAUT TO HEAD NEW TERRAFORMING AGENCY.

Aunt Gloria kept her brother's photograph in a place of pride on top of the piano, and Walt looked at it all the time he was practicing, hoping the colonel would be proud of how well Walt handled the difficult chords in the Mozart piece. His father's steady gray eyes stared back at him from under ruler-straight eyebrows, and his thin lips and square jaw seemed to be challenging Walt to do better.

"I will, Father, I'll make you proud of me," he promised, and wished he looked more like him. Walt had blue eyes under brows that tilted up at the corners, a nose of no particular shape, and a pointy chin nothing like his father's square jaw. He sometimes wondered if he took after his mother. There was no photograph of her at home. Aunt Gloria didn't even know if Father had one, and she would never ask him. Since his mother had died, when Walt was two, his father had never once mentioned her. It was after her death that he had joined the terraforming agency and made his name as a "planet maker."

Walt went to school in Lethbridge, where the other students accepted him as "that weird kid with the father out in space somewhere." He was happy in a quiet way, for in his secret dream life he rode shoulder to shoulder with his father across the landscapes of strange planets.

He rescued his father from innumerable dangers and modestly turned aside his thanks with a shrug and "It was nothing, Dad." Not that he would have called him *Dad* in real life. In his letters he addressed him as "Father," but mostly he thought of him as Aunt Gloria did: my father the colonel.

Life went on very quietly until August 2092. Lethbridge was hot and dry, smelling of sage, the coulees striped with purple shadows. Walt and Aunt Gloria were planning a picnic down along the Oldman River. Walt had left his aunt in the kitchen packing lunch while he strapped the canoe to the car's roof rack. When the phone rang he sat down on the porch steps to wait, hoping it wasn't one of Aunt Gloria's more chatty friends. After awhile he looked impatiently at his watch. The whole day would be spoiled if she didn't hurry up.

He went into the kitchen. She was sitting at the table, the phone clutched in her hand, a look of dismay on her face.

"What is it? What's happened?"

"It's your *father*. Calling all the way from Space Station 423. Oh, Walt, he's furious! Something about a poem, and I can't make head or tail..." She stopped talking in midsentence and began to listen. Walt saw her flush and her eyes get suddenly watery.

"Angus, you're not being fair. This has been Walt's home for *eleven years*. Ever since Lynne died. I've loved him. He's been like a son. You can't just uproot him on a whim."

In the long wait, as her words were transmitted out to the space station, she explained. "He says you're to go and live with him. On some new planet or other. Just like that. After all these years. Walt, I tried to make him listen, but..."

Walt felt his heart give a sudden flip. His imagination soared. To see his *father*. To live with him. To see strange planets. It was what he'd always dreamed of. Wasn't it? Only why was his father so angry? And he'd have to leave Aunt Gloria. And school. Everything. To go out into space.

She was talking again. "Blame me if you want, Angus. But Walt's *not* a sissy. He's growing up into a young man you can be proud of—that Lynne would have been proud of too, I'm sure. Please change your mind, Angus. Give me another chance."

Walt felt his hands get sweaty. He sat down at the table. "Please, can I talk to him?"

"Oh, I don't think that would be wise, dear boy. He's so angry. He says it's time he took over and 'made a man out of you.' That's what he said, so ridiculous!" She sniffed.

The small distant voice of his father quacked in the handset again. Aunt Gloria grabbed the message pad and began to write. Walt looked over her shoulder.

> *Flight 1031 from Los Angeles to Sydney, Australia. Military transport to Wooma-runga Station.*

"Yes, I've got all that. Angus, wait. Listen...Oh, operator, we've been cut off. Yes, I see."

She stared at the handset and then slowly replaced it. "Tomorrow, Walt. You have to go *tomorrow*."

"But..." Panic was making him feel sick. It was all happening too fast. "Aunt Gloria, there won't even be time to get clothes, things I'll need out there."

"They'll outfit you on the station, the colonel said. Walt, I don't understand about this poem. Your father was *furious*."

"I wrote it for his birthday and faxed it to him for a surprise. It cost all my allowance. I thought he'd be pleased. I wanted to do something special, to let him know I...I loved him. Stuff like that," he muttered, feeling his ears get hot. "I didn't know..."

But now he did. Writing poems. Practicing his Mozart for hours to please Aunt Gloria—and his father.

He looked at the photograph on top of the piano. The steady eyes stared back. The jaw jutted and the lips compressed.

I won't write any more poems, Father, he promised the photograph. *I'll make you proud of me. I will. Honest.*

Lying in bed that night, he realized, trembling, that soon he'd be seeing his father, that he'd actually be living in the same house with him. Having breakfast at the same table. It would be awesome, like living with a god.

When at last he fell asleep, he dreamed that he and his father were facing a huge fire-breathing monster on a swampy prehistoric planet. "I'll save you, Dad," he shouted and ran forward, waving his laser gun. But the monster put a foot on his chest and pushed him into the mud. Just before he went under, he saw that the monster had his father's face.

Aunt Gloria flew with him as far as Los Angeles and saw him safely onto the supersonic jet for Sydney, Australia. She hugged him so hard his ribs hurt. "You're *not* a sissy," she whispered fiercely into his hair. "You're a wonderful boy, and I'm so proud of you."

Of course he couldn't cry, not after she'd said that. He gave her a watery smile and a military salute and stepped onto the walkway along with five hundred other passengers, none of whom knew or would have cared that his heart was breaking into little pieces. Would he ever see Aunt Gloria again?

The flight to Sydney lasted through two meals and a movie. Walt ate the food that was put in front of him and stared blankly at the screen. He followed the line of passengers off the plane into the terminal building and was whisked out of the line at Customs and Immigration, then bustled onto a small military jet by a silent man in uniform.

When Walt had got his breath back and unclenched his fists after the takeoff, he looked at the ground far below. *Australia*. He'd studied it in school, of course, but this was real. Green hills grew brown. The land flattened to a vast plain, red, ancient, eroded. A bit like

Lethbridge. Walking from the airport to a waiting jeep was like walking through an oven. A plume of red dust trailed them and the sun was a brassy disk over in the north. The north? Not like Lethbridge. Alien.

His heart thumped as he followed the driver into Woomarunga Station, a collection of white buildings like sugar cubes thrown down on the red dust. He was given a room with a shower, shown the cafeteria, and told to report for a physical. He hoped, for a few wild moments, that the medical officer would find something wrong with him—not anything bad, just enough so he wouldn't have to go into space, so he could go back home.

"A-one." The doctor smiled at him and Walt managed to force his face muscles into something like a smile back. "You're in fine shape. A bit on the skinny side, but that's an advantage. Off you go, son. I envy you. It's a great life out there. Exciting. Hard."

Walt looked out of the window at the tiny upright pencil-line, five kilometers across the desert, that was the rocket, and tried to swallow the lump in his chest. To be launched into space. To face the terrifying unknown. And at the end of his journey, angrily waiting for him, his father the colonel.

The next few weeks were a kaleidoscope of unbelievable impressions all jumbled together. The heat of the sun like a hand slapping him down. Then the roar of rockets. G-forces pressing the breath out of his chest. Afterward the prick of an injection and the helpless fall into sleep, weeks passing heedlessly by as their ship bisected the galaxy. Then consciousness again, the dreamy wakening to the stale smell of recycled air, the feel of his bunk against his back, the noise of their docking at Space Station 423.

The gravity on the space station was low, only about half of Earth's, and when Walt scrambled from his bunk he felt dizzy, wanting to throw up, the queasy feeling of his first roller-coaster ride back in Lethbridge, Alberta, planet Earth. This sensation tended to come back at unexpected moments over the next few hours, as he was outfitted with clothes, but he swore to himself that he'd never give way to it, that he'd always be tough, the way he'd been tough saying good-bye to Aunt Gloria.

Then someone came to tell him that the colonel had arrived, and led him down long curved corridors and into an office. Walt breathed in deeply, sucking in his gut, and stood inside the door, stiff and straight, eyes front, so that his first view of his father was of the colonel's chest and two rows of medal ribbons—just like in the photograph he'd brought with him from home.

"So you're Walt, eh?" His father's voice was unexpectedly gruff.

"Yes, sir."

The colonel cleared his throat. "You're the spitting image of your mother. Welcome aboard, son." His hand shot out, hard and calloused, and Walt tried not to wince in its grip.

"Got your gear?"

"Yes, sir."

"You'll be bunking with me. Can't spare extra space for nonworking personnel. This way."

Walt followed the straight back through a labyrinth of identical passages. His father walked rapidly, decisively, his broad shoulders obscuring the way ahead, until they stopped before one of twenty identical sliding doors. This one bore a temporary tag: COLONEL ANGUS ELLIOT, CHIEF ENGINEER, TERRAFORMING AGENCY.

Walt followed the broad back into the room, put his bag into the closet his father silently indicated, and once more stood at attention.

"At ease," the colonel said. Walt wasn't sure if he was teasing, pretending Walt was one of his men, so he allowed himself to smile as he looked up past the polished buttons and the medal ribbons. The visor of the colonel's cap was a horizontal line slashing his head in two, parallel to the dark eyebrows and the thin unsmiling mouth. Just like the photograph on the piano. But then his expression softened. "Yes, it gave me quite a shock, seeing how like Lynne you look."

"I didn't know. I've never seen a picture of her."

Walt hoped his father would tell him something more about his mother, but instead the colonel went on briskly, "We'll be aboard the station for a couple of days. Then we'll be taking a ship to my next assignment."

"Where's that, sir?" Walt ventured.

"Place called Aqua."

Aqua... "Why?" Walt's curiosity overcame his awe. It was a magic-sounding name.

The colonel frowned. "What do you mean, *why*? Because Earth needs what Aqua's got, which is an ideal soil for the cultivation of oil-bush. Only it needs to be reworked first. That's why I'm going there. That's what I *do*, boy. I should have brought you out sooner, before your aunt had a chance to turn you into one of those bleeding-heart 'don't touch the planet' groupies. Writing poetry's bad enough, but..."

"I didn't mean why are we going there, sir," Walt managed to gasp. "I only meant why is it called Aqua? It's a funny name for a planet," he added feebly.

"Hmm," the colonel grunted, his frown fading. "Not as foolish as some. Sentimental names, like Paradise and Innisfree. As for Aqua, it seems it was discovered by a merchantman with a fancy for *art*." The colonel's voice made it clear to Walt that for him art fell in the same category as poetry. "He called the planet Aquamarine, because of its color from space. Eventually it got shortened to Aqua. Appropriate enough, I suppose. *Aqua* is the Latin for 'water,' and that's about all there is there. At the moment," he added grimly. "That'll change once my crews get moving." His wrist shot out and he glared at his watch. "Lunchtime. I'll show you the way to the cafeteria. After that you're on your own. Keep out of the way. Don't get lost. I've got work to do, checking supply manifests." His father paused in the doorway and looked down at Walt. "We'll have time to get acquainted once we make planetfall. Not accustomed to having a son around," he went on awkwardly. "Don't suppose it's easy for you either."

"No, sir…I mean…it's fine, sir," stammered Walt.

Two months later their supply ship slowly orbited Aqua as they waited their turn for the shuttle down. Walt, with his face pressed against the viewport, saw that Aqua was even bluer than Earth, a paler, wetter blue. Clouds swirled, blurring the shape of the continental masses. Blue-green. The biggest, most beautiful "aggie" in the galaxy.

One of the mariners stopped to look out past his shoulder. "Never changes. I've been ferrying supplies for months now, and I'm still waiting for the clouds to move away and give us a clear day on Aqua."

That was a saying Walt was to become familiar with. "It'll be a sunny day on Aqua" meant the same as "In a blue moon" or "When it rains on Mars"—meaning never.

Aqua looked beautiful from orbit, but the reality of life on the surface was very different. There were hundreds of hectares of low bush and reedy marshland. It didn't rain *all* the time. Sometimes it just drizzled. Once in a great while, they said, it would actually stop drizzling and the clouds would thin so the sun could send a glow of warmth and brightness over the land—so they said. But after the first four days of nonstop rain, Walt thought achingly of the dry heat and the clean westerly winds of Lethbridge. His clothes felt damp all the time.

Books and papers were limp and soggy, and indoors there was a pervasive smell of mildew.

A work crew had already set up prefab houses, a mess hall, surgery, and school on a low hill surrounded by marshland through which meandered several silvery streams. The colonel's house was at the top of the hill, a hundred and fifty meters above the marshland. There was a bedroom for each of them, an office for the colonel, and a small living room that they shared uneasily. They ate in the cafeteria, at a table by themselves, undisturbed by the workers and their families. Looking around enviously at the chattering groups, Walt wondered how he would ever get to know the other kids in the compound.

His second day on Aqua, looking out at the teeming rain from the porch that ran across the front of their house, Walt had never felt so lonely in his life. He even longed for school to start. However strange and different, at least he'd meet the other kids.

His father joined him on the porch, a cup of coffee in hand. "Marvelous, isn't it, son?" He was in a wonderfully relaxed mood and, trying to think of something intelligent to say, Walt peered through the rain at the expanse of marshland. "I...I don't see anything," he ventured.

"That's *it*. Nothing! It's like..." The colonel searched for a simile and failed to find one. "Empty. Waiting for me to start work on it. Shaping it. Making something useful out of it. I tell you, son, there's no job in the galaxy like terraforming."

"What exactly does terraforming mean, Father? What are you going to do?"

"We'll begin by digging canals, so as to drain all this useless water away to the lower ground. Then we'll build dikes to keep it from washing back in. We start with just a small square of land, a piece maybe the size of Prince Edward Island. Then we'll drain the square next to that. And another. Like a patchwork, until we've drained the whole continent and built up the land with the material we've dug out. Then we'll plant oil-bush, build a couple of refineries, and be off to the next planet. It's a marvelous life."

This was the longest conversation Walt had had with his father in the two months he'd known him. It was almost like being friends. He racked his brain for the right thing to say.

"What'll happen to all the water you drain out? Won't it just come back as rain and flood the land again?"

"Good question, son. The scientist joes say that once we've drained the land and planted oil-bush the climate will begin to change. We may have to help out with a couple of controlled nuclear detonations on the other hemisphere to adjust the angle of rotation to the sun, give a bit more variety to the climate. You look surprised. I suppose the old fogies back on Earth have no idea of what we can do, with our new technology."

"Won't that..." Walt stopped, seeing the trap he was about to fall into.

"Go ahead, son. Ask away."

"Well, what I wanted to know was, what about the creatures living here already? What'll happen to them if you change the climate?"

The colonel snorted. "For a start, there *is* no intelligent species on Aqua. As for the rest—who cares? A bunch of frogs and fishes. They can always be replaced by more useful imports from another planet. They're not important. The work's the thing. The remaking."

Fascinated, Walt saw his father's big hands move together, almost as if he were molding a lump of clay. The rain lashed down and a warm mist rose from the swamp. He couldn't think of anything else to say, but if he didn't go on talking his father would go back into his office and he'd be alone out here.

"I just thought of something." He said the first thing that popped into his head, watching the rain come down, rivulets running down the hillside, merging into the reedy swamp below.

"What's that, son?"

"If you take the *l* out of *Walter,* you're left with *water*. Isn't that funny?"

His father stared at him, his face like a granite carving. "What's the significance of that, son?"

"I dunno, Father. Nothing, I guess."

"Nothing comes of nothing." The colonel picked up his coffee mug from the railing and turned toward his office. At the door he turned back. "It's time school started and you got some sense knocked into you."

■ ■ ■

By the end of the first week of school, sporting a split lip, a black eye, and a bruise over his right cheekbone, Walt wondered if maybe his father was psychic. Or maybe he knew something about space schools that Walt didn't. He lay in bed, kept awake by his throbbing cheek, licked his sore lip, and longed to be back in Lethbridge with Aunt Gloria—though she'd have made a fuss over him, and that would have been embarrassing. At least the colonel hadn't made a big deal over the state of his face. Just stopped long enough to say, "Guess you got initiated today. You okay?" And he had lied and said he was fine, that school was great.

School was awful. His favorite subject, English Lit, rated one short hour a week, and the program was laden with computer technology, astronomy, physics, and interplanetary history and geography, subjects they hadn't even touched in eighth grade back home. Math seemed to come into almost everything. He struggled to make sense of his classes and stayed up late every night trying to catch up.

His teacher, Ms. Cunningham, kept him back after class on Friday. "I'm not happy with the way you're failing to adjust, Walt. Your profile rates you as just right for a split eight-nine class, but you're so far behind in most of your subjects, I wonder if you'd be more comfortable back in a six-seven?"

Walt thought of what life would be like among the little kids, with the big kids still beating up on him. "No, please. I promise I'll catch up. I'll work harder. I'll..."

"Okay, okay. No need to panic. I won't give you any extra attention in class, but you can stay for an hour after school each day if you want."

Clear between them was the understanding that the worst thing for Walt would be to be known as Teacher's Pet, as well as being an Earthie *and* the boss's son.

"Thanks," he muttered and left thankfully, even though he knew they would be outside, waiting for him. *They* were Gordon McDuff, Pier Olsen, Li Chung, Paul Ng, and Dylan Williams. All the boys in the class. There were five girls too, but already he knew enough not to pay attention to *them*. He'd learned a lot that first week. Not to boast about his father the colonel. Not to ask questions in class or show off. Not to mention anything about life on Earth. And not to talk to the girls.

But even abiding by all these unwritten laws hadn't helped. The boys, led by Gordon, had been clever and sneaky. They had started on day one with just little things, like putting a foot out so that he tripped on his way to the board and forgot what little trigonometry he knew. Or putting salt on his dessert, so he couldn't eat it and then got scolded by one of the cafeteria staff for wasting food.

On the second day they stole his homework. He never did find out if Ms. Cunningham believed him when he said he'd put it on her desk. On the third day they were waiting for him after school.

"Smart-ass!"

"Think you're someone 'cause you're Earthborn."

"Yeah, and 'cause your dad's the boss."

"Go on. Run home to Daddy and tell him. Dare you."

And all the time they talked they were punching him, one of them holding his arms from behind and the others taking turns, so it wasn't even a fair fight. He tried to knee Gordon, but the others pulled his legs from under him and left him in the mud.

The path up to the top of the hill was deserted, since the day shift was out working on the site and the night shift would still be sleeping, so there was no one to see what had happened, no one except one skinny girl with hair in such tight braids that they stuck out from behind each ear like sticks. She was standing on the porch of the surgery, and she must have seen the whole ignominious affair. Solveig was her name, he remembered. She sat among the girls across the room from him. He picked himself out of the mud and ran up the hill to the colonel's house, his head down, so she wouldn't see his face.

The next day when school was over the same thing happened. Each day he woke up feeling as if he had a huge stone in the middle of his chest. Every day going to school became harder, and concentrating was almost impossible, because he could see them watching him, whispering and grinning at each other, and he knew the beating was going to happen again, and there was absolutely nothing he could do about it.

Then on Friday came Ms. Cunningham's suggestion

about transferring to the six-seven class, and he knew that if things didn't get better soon he'd never catch up. Solveig was swinging on the railing outside the surgery again as he picked himself out of the mud after his tormentors had left.

"Hi," she said, hanging upside down from the railing so that her braids flopped beyond her head. He pretended not to hear.

"I can help if you want," she added, and he found himself stopping. "Judo," she went on. "That's what you need to take care of those guys."

Her voice was totally matter-of-fact, but he felt himself blushing up to his ears and exploded angrily. "I don't need anyone to tell me!" he yelled and plodded up the hill.

But he was desperate enough to tackle the colonel during supper in the cafeteria. "You said they'd knock sense into me at school, Father. Did you know they'd beat me up?"

"Sure." The colonel nodded, shoveling reconstituted meatloaf into his mouth. *Doesn't he care?* Walt wondered.

"Why do they do it? I've really tried to get along."

His father stopped eating and looked straight at him. "I know it's hard, Walt, but that's what life on the frontier's like. Their parents are my employees. I work them damn hard. I go to planets no one else'll touch and I get results. I hire the best and I pay the best, but I make them earn it. It's like the army. I'm commander in chief and they do what I say or else. I'm responsible to no one but the Federation, and it doesn't mess with me. My crews may hate my guts, but they'll never forget working for me. Terraforming a planet under Colonel Elliot is a recommendation they're proud of in spite of the tough life. But they let their kids know what they really think. And the kids take it out on you."

Walt nodded. His split lip and bruised face, not to mention his bruised pride, were just part of the equation that was life on Aqua, something he'd just have to endure.

"Don't you mind them hating you? Wouldn't it go better if they liked you?"

The colonel shook his head vigorously. "I get more out of them my way. You've got to be tough, son, to get along in this galaxy."

The gray eyes were like chips of marble and his hands worked, the way Walt had seen them when he'd been talking about planet reforming. *He sees me like that,* Walt realized. *Like a planet he has to remake.* And he knew that, no matter what happened to him, it was no good running to his father for sympathy. Stubborn anger began to burn inside him. *I'll make him proud of me,* he promised himself.

At the end of the second week of school it hadn't stopped raining once. They were still beating up on him, but Walt got the feeling that maybe they were getting bored. He hoped so. He had a headache most of the time and it was hard to concentrate on classwork and study.

After his catch-up session with Ms. Cunningham on the second Friday, she took him into the cozy staff room and gave him juice and cookies. "I'm sorry you're still getting beat up."

So she knew all the time. But of course she did. She wasn't stupid. Perhaps she had orders too: to make a man of him.

She gave him a wry smile. "Did you think I was blind? Or I didn't care? They're tough kids, born on harsh planets, most of them. You probably can't even imagine what their lives have been like. They envy your coming from Earth, but at the same time they don't want to know about it or acknowledge the kind of homesickness we all have for it. Even humans who left Earth for other planets a generation or more ago regard it as home in a special way. So they envy you for actually having lived there. And the fact that your father's the boss certainly doesn't help."

"Father explained that," he muttered. Not that it was much consolation when a fist came up and bloodied his nose.

"I'm sorry I can't stand up for you publicly, but can you imagine how they'd treat you if I did?"

He understood, and her quiet sympathy filled him with a sudden longing for Aunt Gloria. His eyes filled with tears and he had to reach over for another cookie and cram it in his mouth, even though it nearly choked him.

"They *will* get bored in the end, I promise. It's taking longer than usual because there's so little to do on Aqua. Nowhere to go. This interminable rain . . ."

She sighed, and Walt suddenly realized that he wasn't the only one who hated Aqua. Probably most of them did. They were all in this together. Rain, gray skies, reconstituted food, and all. For some reason this made him feel more cheerful.

"Now, about your work..."

"I *have* tried."

"I know you have. Perhaps too hard. I'm going to forbid you to do more than a couple of hours' homework on weekends. Tell me, what are you interested in? What were your activities back on Earth?"

"Rock climbing. And canoeing and swimming."

She looked out at the watery landscape. "Well, I suppose you *could* swim, but with all those reeds it wouldn't be much fun. What about hobbies?"

"I love reading, but there are no books here except school ones."

"I have a few you can borrow, if you promise to be careful with them."

"Oh, yes." The stone seemed to shrink and he felt lighter already. "I studied piano back on Earth, but I don't think Father...and I like writing too. I write...I *used* to write poetry," he blurted, and instantly wished he hadn't. He'd have taken back the words if he could. But it was all right. She smiled sympathetically.

"I won't tell a soul about the poetry. But why don't

you explore Aqua, what there is of it, on weekends? Find out all you can. Keep a journal, maybe."

"I suppose..."

"You see, Walt, if the others see you busy, enjoying yourself and not bothering about them, maybe they'll stop despising you and begin to respect you. I can't promise, but it's worth a try."

He flinched at the word *despise*. But that was more or less what his father had said, wasn't it? They hated the colonel and despised his son. Well, he'd show them.

"That girl, Solveig, said she'd teach me judo."

"You could certainly do worse than have her as a friend. In a way you're in the same boat, you know. Her mother's the camp doctor and in a privileged position too. Her father's working somewhere else in the Federation. I'd guess she may be just as lonely as you are."

He hadn't thought of her as lonely. She always looked so self-sufficient, swinging from the surgery porch and watching everyone else go by with an aloof expression on her face. Perhaps that was her way of coping.

"Can you manage another cookie?" Ms. Cunningham said, interrupting his thoughts. "Sure? Well, off you go then, and good luck."

Her smile warmed him and, best of all, when he closed the school door behind him, he found that the others had got tired of waiting for him and had gone off. He glanced at his watch and remembered that its time made no sense on Aqua, with its slightly faster daily rotation. Nearly suppertime, anyway. There was no one around, except for Solveig, swinging on the surgery porch railing. He almost stopped to say hi, but then he felt suddenly shy and ran up the hill to the colonel's house without stopping. He felt almost happy for once. It was like a good omen, not getting punched.

I'll explore and make maps, as well as keep a journal, he told himself. *I'll make Aqua mine, the way Lethbridge and the Oldman River used to be.*

TWO

Walt began his exploration of Aqua from the porch of his father's house.

He wrote on the first page of his new journal:

> From the top of the hill the compound's built on, I can see for a long way in every direction, the country's so flat. To the north it's all marshland, with little rivers running through it. This is where the work's beginning. Huge machines gouging out the river bottoms and piling the dirt up on top, to drain the marsh and raise the land level.
>
> All day long and into the night we can hear the noise of the machines, like a kind of low rumbling thunder. Nights are dark on Aqua, with no moon or stars showing through the clouds, but over in the north

the lights of the machines turn night into day. It doesn't look bright and cheerful, the way you might think, because of the black mud everywhere. The machines and the men and women operating them are covered with mud from head to foot. They keep putting down walkways of plastic stuff across the marsh, but they're soon covered with mud too.

Over to the northwest is a flat, drier area, and that's where the shuttles land. One of them is still there, like a stubby bullet standing on its end. There are huts not far away. Communications and stuff like that, I guess. Civilians aren't allowed anywhere near there, so this is probably the best view I'll get of it.

My bedroom faces the other way, toward the south. The view is nicer, because due south of here is another hill, bigger than this one, rocky and covered with greenery. I suppose this hill was like that once, but it's been lasered down to bedrock for all the houses and stuff. I think I'll start exploring that way tomorrow.

He woke at first light on Saturday, but the colonel had already left, so he had a quick breakfast by himself in the cafeteria and wheedled a packed lunch out of the staff. Then, dressed in the now-familiar yellow rain gear of hooded jacket, pants, and high boots, he set out.

"A fine day, for Aqua," the kitchen helper had told him, which meant that it wasn't actually raining, just a small drizzle prickling his face. Looking around, he felt a sudden stab of homesickness for the river valley back home, all purple and red in the sun, and the clean dry air with the heady scent of sagebrush as the day heated up. But at least, over there in the south, where the engineers hadn't yet started work, Aqua looked clean and peaceful.

To the north the land was like a sore, the kind of sore that doesn't heal properly. It made him feel angry and sick, and he turned his back on it and walked down the hill from the compound in the opposite direction and set out along the single walkway that spanned the distance between this hill and the one to the south.

His boots made no sound on the plastic, but the walkway itself bounced a little under his weight and made a faint sucking sound against the marshy ground over which it had been laid. It was a funny feeling, like walking across the surface of a giant trampoline, and he had to concentrate on keeping a steady course and not overbalancing into the muddy water. He found, after walking unsteadily for a while, that looking dead ahead of him toward the hill helped.

He strode along, humming to himself, until the watery world seemed to turn suddenly upside down, and he found himself lying face down on the smooth plastic, his hands smarting from the impact, the breath pushed out of his body. He struggled to get the air back into his lungs, as the familiar knot clenched his stomach. Had Gordon and the others somehow got out here ahead of him and lain in wait on purpose to trip him up? He lay tensely, waiting for a punch or a kick in the ribs. Nothing happened, and when he looked up there was no one in sight.

Lying on his stomach on the walkway, he found he had a new and interesting view of Aqua. The reeds, growing in the marshy soil and on the edges of the rivulets that flowed through it, were about a handspan apart, straight, greeny-gold, their tips powdery with golden pollen. They looked like a forest of yellow paint-brushes stuck, tips upward, into the mud. Some aquatic creature splashed nearby. He wondered if his father had ever lain on his stomach and looked at Aqua in this particular way.

After awhile he sat up, rubbing his stinging hands together. What on earth was it that had tripped him? There seemed to be nothing but smooth plastic under-foot. He noticed that a long strand of grass had caught in the fastening of his boot, and he pulled it free and was just about to toss it aside when something caught his eye. Curiously he ran the strand through his fingers. That was weird. It wasn't just any old piece of grass, but a long looped string made of several strands of fiber twisted together. Possibly, just possibly, that might have happened by accident. But the string had then been knotted or twisted into a kind of lacy pattern. Definitely a pattern. And for him to have tripped because of it, it must have been fastened to the reeds at ankle height and stretched across the walkway to the reeds on the other side.

He sat staring at it, his heart pounding against his ribs, while the significance of his find slowly sank in. An intelligent being had twisted and knotted this length of string and fastened it across the walkway. But there were no intelligent beings on Aqua—everybody had told him that. Only humans. And a human wouldn't bother to make a string out of *grass*. He'd just requisition some polyfiber from supply.

Then he noticed something else odd. At the place where his foot had become entangled in the string, the walkway was sagging, so that water was beginning to seep over its edges. That shouldn't be happening. One of the things he'd learned since he'd arrived on Aqua was that this kind of plastic was one of the strongest synthetics in the galaxy. The colonel had boasted about its properties and explained exactly how his engineers had injected piers of the material deep into the marshes and laid the walkways over them. "They'll last forever," he had boasted.

But when Walt reached out to touch the walkway, it felt sludgy, like a piece of half-melted toffee. A sudden burning pain made him draw his hand back quickly and stare at it. The tips of the fingers of his left hand were red and beginning to blister. He dunked them quickly in the water beside the walkway and swished them around to wash off whatever had caused the burn. It felt like acid. But where could it have come from?

He was still kneeling, cooling his burning hand in the water, when he caught a sudden movement in the corner of his eye. He blinked it into focus and, just for a second, thought he saw a face framed in the reeds, a green face with wide amber eyes set slantingly under a broad, low forehead. Then it was gone and he was left staring, open-mouthed, at the endless rows of reeds standing straight and stiff until, in the distance, they seemed to crowd so closely you could no longer see between them.

Their powdery pollen heads didn't stir. The water between the stalks was as smooth as glass. There was no sound anywhere but Walt's heavy breathing. *Did I see something?* he wondered. There was certainly nothing now to tell him he hadn't imagined that alien face. There was nothing but the blisters on his fingertips and the strangely knotted string. He got slowly to his feet and looked toward the distant hill he had been aiming for. Exploring it seemed kind of meaningless now, after what he'd just seen. His head whirling, he walked slowly back toward the compound, wondering who he could ask. Who could explain? Certainly not his father. He cringed as he pictured the scene. "Knotted grasses? Faces in the reeds? My son, the raving idiot!"

The same problem would face him if he talked to Solveig. If they were already friends it might be different—she might even believe him. Ms. Cunningham?

For a moment he thought of confiding in her; but in spite of cookies and sympathy she was still an Agency employee. She might feel it her duty to tell his father. No, he had nobody he could trust.

Maybe he could get some information from the scientists on Aqua, without letting them know why he wanted it. They worked in a couple of small buildings labeled "Research" and kept very much to themselves. Walt knew that his father contemptuously called them "eggheads," because they only used their brains instead of getting their hands dirty. Up till then Walt hadn't talked to any of them, but now he walked over and went boldly up to the door of the main building and pushed it open.

Inside he saw a bewildering collection of electron microscopes, spectral-analysis readers, computers, and busy, clean-looking men and women in dazzling white coats. It was the cleanest place on Aqua.

"Get that muddy gear outta here," someone screamed at him, as he hesitated on the threshold. He noticed then that he was hovering on the edge of a kind of mud room, hung with coats and boots. Apologetically he scrambled out of his rain gear, donned a white coat and white overshoes, and, rather self-consciously, went into the main room.

"That's better," said the man who'd screamed at him. "Any contamination could ruin our experiments. What can I do for you?"

"Can I talk to a biologist?" Walt asked, having

worked out what he wanted to say on his way back to the compound.

"Over there." The man indicated a woman whose bright coppery hair curled crisply over the top of her head. "Her name's Samantha. She won't bite unless you call her 'carrots.'"

Recognizing a joke, Walt smiled feebly and picked his way across the crowded lab to where the red-haired woman was working.

"Please?"

"Hmm?"

"I'm confused about the animals on Aqua. I haven't seen anything much, not even an insect."

"You're from Earth, aren't you? The colonel's son? Right. You've got to understand that the morphology of Earth fauna is not necessarily reflected in that of other planets, even ones with similar characteristics."

"Huh?"

She looked at him properly then, running a hand through her hair so that it stood straight up in a carroty halo. "Goodness, whatever have you done to your face? It looks as if it's been trampled on."

Walt's hand went up to his bruised eye and cheek. "S'nothing. What was that about morph…something?"

"Sorry. I wasn't paying attention. What I mean is that the way animals developed on Earth, from single-celled organisms through the primitive slimes to diatoms, larger water creatures without skeletons like jellies and slugs, and creatures with exoskeletons like crustacea and internal skeletons like fish, and so on up to land animals, isn't necessarily the way they've developed in other places, especially those with unusual climates, like Aqua. Here the fauna is totally dependent on water, so there are only fishlike creatures and amphibians..."

"Like frogs, you mean?"

"Like, but not the same. There is a large variety of frog- and salamander-like creatures, almost as varied as the insect population on Earth. But they haven't had the time, or perhaps the opportunity, to get beyond that stage."

"Does that mean there's no intelligent life on Aqua?"

Samantha looked shocked. "Of course it does. We wouldn't be here if there were. Don't you know the Federation laws about extraterrestrial life?"

"Like the one that says we can't land on any planet that's already got an established intelligent life form, unless they ask us? And we can't terraform any planet that's got a life form on its way to becoming intelligent?"

"That's right. But you see, there are only nonintelligent species on Aqua, so the Agency has permission to terraform it. That means, in this case, to drain the swamps, change the climate, and plant oil-bush."

"But..."

"What's the problem?" She was frowning now, looking back at her work.

"On Earth there are whales and dolphins, living in the sea but superintelligent. Talking to each other..."

"Mammals, not amphibians. That's the big difference. There is no known planet on which an amphibian has been anything but an early step on the long way up toward higher intelligence. Why, if we weren't absolutely sure of that, we wouldn't have got a license to terraform Aqua, would we?"

"No, I suppose not." Walt hesitated for a minute, wondering whether to show her the knotted twine and tell her about the face in the reeds, but she had already turned back to her work. He thanked her and left the lab. Dressed once more in his rain gear, he plodded up to the top of the hill. As he passed the surgery he saw Solveig out on the porch.

"Hi," she called. "Where've you been?"

He felt his ears getting red. "Just around," he muttered and walked on.

His father wasn't home, of course. It might be Saturday, but that didn't mean time off for the workers or their boss. He looked at the clock. Not even lunchtime yet. For the rest of the day he prowled restlessly around the small house, his mind stuck in a round-and-round argument. An intelligent being had made and knotted that piece of string. But if there were any intelligent beings on Aqua, his father wouldn't be allowed to terraform the planet.

If only he had a friend to talk to, a logical person who could explain where his argument had gone wrong, he'd feel better. Around and around it went in his brain. The picture of the calm amber eyes staring at him kept flashing back into his mind. His face got hot and his head ached.

He spread the knotted string out on the table. It had come unlooped in his pocket and now he tried to reconstruct the way he thought the knots and loops had twined into each other. It was rather like a cat's cradle. When he thought he'd got it right, he drew the pattern in his journal and slipped the string into a plastic envelope for safekeeping. Someday, maybe, he'd show it to someone and prove that he wasn't entirely crazy.

I ought to show it to Father, he thought. *Once he understands that someone intelligent made it, he'll have to stop work.*

He'll never believe me, another voice said scornfully. *He'll say I did it myself. And I don't have any proof I didn't.*

If I could find another clue and show him, maybe...?

He'll never leave, the negative voice said. *Not till he's made Aqua into what he wants it to be. Nothing I can say or do will change his mind. And he'd be mad at me. He'd say I was no good.*

That was the bottom line, wasn't it? To have Father accept him. Easier to pretend that nothing had happened, that it was all in his imagination. So when the colonel came in, covered with mud and happy as a clam after a fruitful day spent gouging into the mud of Aqua, he hid the envelope under his pillow. When his father asked him what he'd been doing all day he muttered, "Nothing much."

As soon as the words were out, he realized that was the wrong thing to say. Not that Father said anything. He just *looked*, and Walt knew he was thinking what a useless son he had. And of course the problem wouldn't go away, even though he tried to push it out of his head. He couldn't sleep. Late in the night he wandered into the living room and looked out. The rain had begun again and was coming down in curtains of shimmering white, blurring the lights of the excavators. What would it be like to live out there in the marshes, among the reeds? What would it be like to grow up never seeing the sun, never feeling the comforting warmth of a fire? He shivered, though it wasn't cold, went back to his room, and snuggled down in bed, his head under the blanket.

On Sunday morning the worrying question was still there, like a sore tooth, niggling at his mind as soon as he woke up. Father had already gone to the work site. Walt had a quick breakfast in the cafeteria and then waded through the pouring rain to the computer center. He found an empty terminal and accessed ALIEN SPECIES: INTELLIGENT.

There was a lot of information. As he flipped through the data, scrolling up screen after screen, looking at the pictures, reading the occasional word, it seemed that Samantha had been dead right. Only terrestrially based animals appeared to possess the kind of intelligence that counted. But how do you measure intelligence? If you lived most of the time under water, on a very wet planet, you couldn't use fire; you wouldn't be able to work metals, or make paper and keep written records.

He stopped reading the screen as something suddenly nudged at his mind; nothing came of it and he went on. Even language would be difficult, he realized, remembering swimming lessons in the Lethbridge pool, making faces under water at another kid and trying to talk. Managing only bubbly noises before running out of breath. On the other hand, whales could certainly communicate with each other, and they were certainly intelligent. But that hadn't stopped Earth people from almost wiping them out for important reasons like steaks, margarine, and explosives. His mind was a muddle and nothing he could find out made it any clearer.

Time was going by, and he had homework to finish before Monday. He ran back through the rain and found his father enjoying a rare moment's rest, his feet up on the railing of the porch, a can of beer in his hand. It was pouring so hard now, he told Walt, that work on the project had had to be halted. "I've got the crews busy in the sheds repairing and overhauling machinery. We can have some time together."

He sounded friendly, the way Walt had hoped a father would be. "That'll be great." He wanted to add "Dad," but he couldn't quite manage it. He sat on the porch rail, swinging his legs.

"Father?"

"Yes, son?"

"Suppose you suddenly found there *was* an intelligent species on Aqua, what would you do?"

"Execute my chief biologist." The colonel laughed, but Walt could almost see him doing it.

"No, seriously."

"It couldn't happen."

"Just suppose. Suppose the survey team made a mistake. Would you stop?"

The colonel's straight eyebrows drew together until they made a black slash across the top of his face. "I don't turn my back on a job. Not ever. Has anyone told you differently?"

"N-no, sir."

"Good. Just you remember that, Walter. When your father puts his hand to terraforming a planet, that planet bends to his will. Nothing, absolutely *nothing*, gets in the way. Clear?"

"Yes, sir."

"Let me tell you about some of the other jobs I've had to do, jobs no one else would handle, that they said were impossible. I carved the tops off the mountains on Prometheus and pulverized the rocks. Turned a useless hunk of stone into the largest agricultural planet in that quadrant of the galaxy. I gouged through the ranges of Ethos so the useless waters of the inland sea could reach the inhabited coastal plains."

Walt looked at his father sprawled in his chair, his feet on the railing, and glowed with pride. He remembered how, when he was a little kid, he'd thought his father was like a god. And it was true: his father was godlike, remaking whole worlds. His very own father. "Go on, tell me some more."

His father talked, spinning tales of fiery planets, of

impenetrable jungles, of carnivorous beasts whose fangs dripped poison. He talked of being trapped in the pull of giant stars, of being squeezed by forces of gravity, of being marooned and left for dead. He was like all the heroes of Walt's childhood reading and TV-watching rolled into one. He was Superman and King Arthur.

Neither of them noticed the dull day slowly darken into cloud-covered night until the colonel suddenly swung his feet down from the railing and exclaimed, "I'm starving! Look at the time, boy. We've missed dinner."

It turned out not to be a tragedy, but the perfect end to an amazing day. The colonel took Walt down to the cafeteria and unlocked the back door. Together they raided the cupboards and refrigerators until they had a tray piled high with food.

"Is it really all right?" Walt hesitated over a piece of pie.

"Take it, son. I'm head of this project and my word is law on this planet. Take two pieces if you want."

Walt chuckled as he carried the laden tray back to the house. His father lit a candle and they had a cozy meal, their first real meal together, sitting on cushions on either side of the coffee table. Then his father had a couple more beers and went on talking.

Finally Walt dared to ask this new, amazingly approachable father something that had been bugging him since he was a kid, something Aunt Gloria had never been able to help him understand.

"My mother..." He hesitated.

"You want to know about her?"

"What she was like, Father. Everything."

The colonel got abruptly to his feet and strode into his room. For a minute Walt's heart plunged. He should have kept quiet. Now he'd done it, ruined a great evening.

But it was all right. The colonel came back and silently held out to Walt a small picture in a duralite frame. Blue eyes under quirky brows, and a small pointy chin. *Hello, Mom,* said Walt silently, recognizing himself. Looking at the picture gave him an oddly reassuring feeling of belonging that he'd never had before, good and loving though Aunt Gloria had been. In this picture his mother was very young, younger than Ms. Cunningham and years younger than Aunt Gloria. But of course she would be. The photograph must be over eleven years old.

The colonel reached over and took the picture from Walt's hand. "Don't really know why I keep it," he said. "With the frame it weighs close to fifty grams. Every time I pack my belongings for a new assignment I figure on throwing it out. But somehow it always gets tucked in my gear." He ran his thumb absently around the edge of the frame in a gesture that was like a caress.

"What happened to her?" Walt asked timidly.

"You mean—how did she die? I was in the regular Planetary Service then. We'd just been transferred to Saturnis Five. A nasty climate, wet, tropical, with leeches dropping on you from the trees and insects swarming so thick it was hard to eat without getting a mouthful. *You* thrived there, oddly enough. You were a tough little guy at eighteen months. But Lynne got thinner and thinner until she just faded away. No stamina." He sounded angry, almost as if it were her fault.

"So you sent me home to Aunt Gloria?"

"Mistake, that. She's a nice enough woman, my sister, I suppose, but woolly-headed. Always was. Remember when we were kids she'd cry her eyes out over a dead mouse, a beetle even." He smiled, a real smile that for an instant changed his whole face. "I used to arrange great funerals for Gloria's dead creatures. Full military honors, bugle playing the Last Post and everything. But Gloria would always spoil it by spouting poetry."

Walt felt himself flinch and, quick as a spear, his father's eyes were on him. "You been writing any more of that poetry since you've been here?"

"N-no, sir."

"That's good. You look a whole lot like Lynne. Shook me when I first saw you, to tell you the truth. But I don't want you growing up like her. She was too gentle. Too soft."

"It wasn't *her* fault she died, Father."

"I know that, boy. But if she'd only been a bit tougher... Though Saturnis Five was a bad place. Not really fit for human habitation. It was then I made the decision that humans shouldn't have to tolerate conditions like that. That we ought to be able to clean up the planets we moved in on, turn them into decent places to live. I joined the terraforming agency and worked my way up to the top."

Walt took this in, puzzled over it, and then blurted out, "But no one's going to live on Aqua, are they?"

"That's true. Only a few agronomists looking after the oil-bush. The refinery will be automated. Then there'll be cargo ships coming in for the oil, once it's running smoothly."

"So you terraform two kinds of planet, is that right? Ones for humans to colonize and others just for raw material?"

"That's how it's worked out over the last ten years. Makes no difference to me. Either way it's war: me and my equipment against It."

"It?"

"The planet. I don't care what it throws at me, what kind of killer planet it is. I'm going to win. Swore I would after Lynne's death. And I always have. Always will." His father got slowly to his feet, nodded good night, and went to his room, taking the photograph of Walt's mother with him. As he passed Walt he touched his shoulder lightly. "Good talking to you, son."

His head spinning with all the information he'd got, one way or another, over this strange weekend, Walt wandered off to his own room. As he finally fell into bed he realized that he never had finished his homework; somehow it didn't bother him the way it would have the week before.

He lay in bed, glowing with pride at being Colonel Elliot's son. It was a responsibility that seemed to have more to do with being strong and having a single purpose, and not so much with getting a hundred percent in trigonometry or space science, though that was important too.

He snuggled under his blanket, promising himself that he wasn't going to be afraid of Gordon and his friends, or let them bully him anymore. He'd show them, just as Father would. He wouldn't be weak, not he. He turned on his side and slipped his hand under the pillow by his neck. His fingers touched something smooth and firm. Puzzled, he drew it out and felt the square shape in the dark. It was the plastic envelope he'd put the mysterious string into the evening before.

That's what had been niggling at his mind down at the computer center. Could the cat's cradle pattern be a kind of communication? For a moment his doubts came whirling back: then he told himself firmly, *Father knows about Aqua. There isn't any intelligent life. I'm just being stupid.* He opened his window wider and shook out the open envelope, so that the twisted, knotted string fell down into the wet darkness outside. Then he lay down again and went straight to sleep.

THREE

As she had promised, Ms. Cunningham gave him the run of her books, and he found a wonderful old collection of short stories called *The Martian Chronicles* and a modern anthology by Thomas Tarian. There were aliens in both sets of stories, strange wise beings out of the past. In an odd way they made the amber-eyed face and the pattern of twisted twine more unlikely, like something out of a story too. Just my imagination, Walt told himself, as he walked down to Ms. Cunningham's house the next Friday evening to give the books back.

They were waiting for him. Gordon, Paul, Li, Dylan, and Pier. "Where d'you think you're going, Earthie?"

"What you got there?"

If they spoil her books I'll kill them, Walt thought, and backed up against the wall of a nearby house, so they couldn't get behind him. He shoved the books into the safety of his raincoat and fought them off with fists and feet. He would have lost in the end, but someone opened a window and yelled at them and they made off, leaving Walt to lick his sore knuckles and go on his way. The pain almost didn't bother him. *Father would be proud of me,* he thought, feeling good clear through.

They won't try that again, I bet. Maybe they'd even become friends of a sort, if they were all together on Aqua for long enough. That would be okay.

But on Saturday morning he was glad to be off on his own, a packed lunch and a water bottle in one pocket, sketch pad and pencil in the other. The day stretched out in front of him and he had a new planet to explore and map. Maybe this was how his father had felt when he had first set out to terraform alien planets.

Solveig was on her porch watching him as he went by. For a second he hesitated. She looked lonely, swinging on the porch railing, and he remembered guiltily what Ms. Cunningham had said about her; but today was *his* day, he argued. *His* adventure. He walked on by and soon forgot about her, thinking of his great day ahead.

He swung along the walkway leading south, taking long confident strides, slowing down only when he came to the place where he'd found the knotted string. Not that he was interested in who or what had made the knots; he'd worked out in his mind that it was probably nesting material for some creature. After all, weavers and hummingbirds built intricate nests—didn't they?—weaving them together with their bills from some predetermined wiring in their tiny brains.

But he was interested in the gummy area of plastic. He should have mentioned it to his father the other night, but, swept away on the torrent of his father's stories, he had forgotten all about it until just now. Luckily nobody used this walkway, since the work was all going on in the north. It had got much worse in the last week. The plastic had sagged beneath the water and appeared to be disintegrating into sticky strings like cheese on a pizza. The damaged area was now more than a meter across, luckily not too far to jump. He took a run at it and cleared it easily, feeling the walkway bounce and buckle under his feet. He *must* remember to tell the colonel on his return.

As he strode along the plastic walk, to the left and right he caught occasional glimpses of silvery water meandering downward from the hill ahead. It would be fun to explore by boat, he thought. There must be something useful down at the work site. Dories perhaps. Or canoes. If the reeds weren't too thick to paddle through.

By the time he had reached the dry land at the base of the hill, the position of Aqua's sun in the sky and the empty feeling in his stomach both told him that it must be lunchtime. He climbed partway up the hill and found a comparatively dry rocky spur surrounded by the low lush vegetation of Aqua, and unwrapped his sandwiches. He was getting almost accustomed to space fare, which, even when it was disguised as "steak" or "pie," tended to taste the same. Filling, anyway.

He found himself vividly remembering the last picnic he'd had with Aunt Gloria, down at Writing-on-Stone Park back in Alberta. Among the hoodoos they had had fried chicken and potato salad and pickles, tomatoes warm out of the garden, and squares of Aunt Gloria's special carrot cake. He took a swig of flat-tasting boiled water and wondered sadly how Aunt Gloria was managing without him.

But this wasn't how his father had got to be head of the terraforming agency—by brooding over the past, he told himself firmly. He repacked the bottle and the wrapper from his sandwich and began to draw the view to the north from his vantage point. Streams flowing down the hillside had gouged three distinct channels in the marsh, and he could trace their glittering meanders through the valley, around the hill where the compound had been built, and out of sight into the mist.

When he'd finished this first sketch to his satisfaction he got to his feet and set off uphill. He decided he'd make another sketch from the crest of the hill, and then see what lay beyond it to the south. He stayed on the dry, higher ground, noticing that the streams became narrower to right and left as he climbed. He guessed they would soon vanish into the ground.

The day was comfortably warm and here, on the luxuriant growth of the hill, he smelled pleasant herby scents, different from anything he'd smelled before. *What a pity,* he thought, *that the engineers have scraped all the vegetation from the other hill before laying down the plastic walkways and putting up the prefab buildings of the compound.* He had no idea that Aqua could smell so...so magical.

It had been a long time since he'd had a chance to really stretch his legs, and he climbed steadily, enjoying the tug at his calf muscles, the taste of the unpolluted air he sucked deep into his lungs, and the quietness, removed as he was from the incessant rumble of terraforming machinery and the explosions of laser charges that had become a daily background noise on Aqua.

He walked with his head high, his legs and arms moving in a steady rhythm, his calves brushing against low shrubby growth. When his right foot slipped suddenly downward he threw his weight forward to compensate. But instead of his left foot meeting solid ground, it met nothingness. For a breathtaking instant his hands grabbed for a safe hold and found nothing but leaves. His heart lurched as they came away in his hands. He fell, and went on falling, down into profound darkness.

Slowly Walt regained consciousness. He was lying on his back on something hard and bumpy, and he was hurting worse than he'd ever hurt in his life, including when he'd been thrown the first time Aunt Gloria had taken him horseback riding. After a time the pain began to focus in his back and ribs. He opened and shut his fingers and found that he could move his arms.

But what about his legs? He'd read somewhere that

if you couldn't feel your legs, then your back was broken. He hoped that wasn't true. But it was all right; he told his toes to wiggle and they did. He breathed a deep sigh of relief and then yelled out, because his chest hurt as if knives were being jabbed into his ribs.

His voice sounded unfamiliar, echoing, as if he were in a very high-roofed building, like a church—no, larger than that, like a cathedral. He opened his eyes a slit. Directly above him, like a pale moon, hovered a small gray disk. A moon? He'd never seen Aqua's moon. He frowned and closed his eyes again, trying to puzzle out what had happened to him. Slowly it came back: his slipping foot, his hands wildly clutching, and the sensation of falling.

With a sick feeling in his stomach he realized what the gray moon disk really was. Its rim gave him a peephole view of the cloudy sky of Aqua; it must be the hole he had fallen through. It was only the size of a dime. That must mean that it was a long way up and there was probably no way of climbing back.

Sinkhole. The word floated up from his memory of an adventure story set in England's Peak district. The hero had fallen through a sinkhole—a place where the ground had collapsed—and discovered an elaborate cave system underground. But in the story his best friend had seen him fall. Nobody had seen Walt. Nobody on Aqua knew he was here. Nobody would even miss him until suppertime, maybe not even then. Maybe not till Sunday.

I wish I'd talked to Solveig, he thought. *Told her where I was going.* Had she seen which way he'd gone? Would she have cared?

He clenched his fists and forced his eyes open again, so that he could see just how bad things were. The hole really was like a moon, and when he turned his head slightly he thought he could see stars. A dark sky studded with hundreds upon hundreds of stars. But that made absolutely no sense at all. It was early afternoon when he'd fallen through the hole. Surely it couldn't be night already? He didn't think he'd been unconscious for *that* long. Anyway, even if he was seeing the night sky, it wouldn't look like this. He was on Aqua, not Earth, and Aqua would be covered with clouds. It always was. He decided he must be seeing things. He'd probably hit his head in the fall. "Seeing stars"—that was it.

He blinked, shifting his eyes cautiously from left to right, but the stars didn't go away. They crowded the darkness overhead. Slowly he began to realize that the constellations and clusters of light he saw were encrusted on the roof of the cave he had fallen into. They seemed to glow and pulse with life against the black velvet of the background. It was very beautiful.

He tried to sit up, rolling onto his left side and pushing himself up cautiously on his elbow. There was another stabbing pain, as well as a solid ache that was probably only bruises, all down his left side. He would be all right, he decided, if he remembered not to breathe too deeply.

His exploring hands met small rocks and stones slimed over with moisture. He guessed that he was sitting on the top of a small hillock, probably made up of debris that had fallen through the hole above his head. All around the hillock was a sea of blackness. It was like a reflection of the night sky in a dark mirror, because it too blazed with stars. He slid carefully to the bottom of the mound and reached out his right hand. As his brain registered *cold* and *wet,* the stars broke into shards and shimmers of dazzling white. He drew back his hand and stared. Slowly the ripples subsided and the star patterns were back.

What had happened to him now became clear. Not very good news. Not good at all. He realized that he had fallen onto a tiny islet in the middle of an underground lake of unknown size. Above him, a long way off, cave walls reached up and curved in toward the hole he had fallen through. He had absolutely no way of telling if there was another way out, or in which direction it might lie.

He shivered and clasped his arms around his knees. He was cold and he was scared and there was nothing he could do. He had no idea how long he crouched there in the darkness, his mind racing around in circles like a gopher in a cage. Then, slowly, something began to happen. It was like hearing a kind of music, except it was not *out there,* but inside his head.

Courage, the music seemed to say. *You will get out.*

Maybe I'll be missed, Walt thought hopefully. *Maybe*

Solveig saw me go and told Father. Then he'll organize a search party.

But the trapped-gopher part of his mind whined: *They'll never find you. The odds of finding the sinkhole are tiny. And infrared scanners won't show up your body heat through all this rock. Not a chance.*

If he could light a signal fire, he thought, the smoke would go up that sinkhole like a chimney. They'd be sure to see it back at the site. He felt around him for small sticks, something to start a fire. But there was nothing within reach of his groping fingers but stones glued together with mud.

And you don't have a lighter anyway, said the despairing inner voice.

After a time he decided that, given the choice of sitting on his rock pile till he starved or trying to get away and maybe drowning, he'd sooner drown. If there were any currents in the water, they might possibly show him a way out. He tore his lunch wrapper into tiny pieces and floated them on the water. They glimmered in the reflected light of the "stars" overhead and, now that his eyes had adjusted to the almost total darkness, he could follow their progress as they drifted slowly away. There were two currents, it seemed, one at right angles to the other. He decided to follow the stronger. If he got lucky it might lead him to an opening in the hill, perhaps the source of one of the streams that flowed down into the marsh. Perhaps the opening would be big enough for him to crawl through. Maybe.

He struggled out of his rain gear, gasping at the pain in his side, and, stripped to his undershirt and shorts, slid slowly into the water. It was cool, but not unpleasantly so. His feet slithered over slippery stones and he walked cautiously forward. He was almost instantly over his head, coughing and spluttering.

He righted himself and swam cautiously through the star reflections into the blackness beyond. It was like swimming through ink. He had the feeling that when—if—he ever came out into daylight again, his whole body would be dyed with its blackness. Turning his back on the only solid, familiar place in this underground world was terrifying, but he told himself firmly that the light from the sinkhole was there, overhead, like a beacon, in case he lost his sense of direction. He swam grimly on into the darkness, following the faint flecks of sandwich wrapping.

Unexpectedly his foot touched bottom. He stood up, shoulder deep, and tried to feel the tug of the current against his body. This direction? Or that? He swam a little farther. Waist-deep now. He stood up again and strode confidently forward. Two strides later he smacked into solid rock. Lights danced behind his eyes. He clutched his head and whimpered. His voice came back to him close, as if he were shut in a closet. He felt trapped and lashed out, bruising his knuckles against slimy stone. Around his knees the current flowed swiftly toward the rock face, forcing its way out through a dozen fissures. Soon it would be part of the stream trickling down the hillside outside. But there was no way through there for *him*.

He wanted to cry. He longed for the matter-of-fact comfort of Aunt Gloria. He forced himself to turn and begin to make his way back. It was much harder swimming against the current; he hadn't thought of that before. He swam a slow awkward breaststroke toward the star reflections on the water, but his side hurt dreadfully and the lights didn't seem to be getting any closer. Just ten more strokes, he told himself. Then ten more, and I'll be able to see the light from the sinkhole. He forced his body forward and at last he was once more swimming in the starry water; there, above him, was the pale moon-disk of the hole. Another few strokes and he grazed his knees on rock and slowly dragged himself back onto his islet.

He was safe for the moment, but back where he started and no better off. Was it his imagination, or was the pale gray circle above his head growing darker? How long had he lain unconscious after his fall? How long had it taken him to swim to the cave wall and back? Time and space seemed to lose all meaning in this shapeless dark. Sooner or later, though, night would fall on Aqua. In total darkness he wouldn't be able to find his way out of this cave even if he were staring right at an opening.

He sat hunched on his pile of rocks, struggling to swallow his panic. What would Father do if this happened to him? He wouldn't give up, that was for sure.

Walt shivered and wondered if it would be worthwhile putting his rain gear back on. At least he'd be warm. Then he wondered why he was shivering. *It's not just being scared,* he thought. *My left side's definitely colder than my right. That's a draft I'm feeling. On my wet skin. Fresh air.*

He stared to his left, the opposite direction to the one he had explored before. There was nothing in the blackness but the high arch of "stars." It seemed to be higher on that side, he noticed. As if maybe the roof itself was higher. Maybe leading up. Leading out.

Without giving himself time to think or to argue himself out of it, he slid once again into the water and began to swim with slow careful strokes through the star reflections toward the center of the arch of blackness. Another stroke. Another. His toes grazed rock. He felt and found a shelf of dry land. He climbed up, took a couple of steps forward, and instantly tripped over something hard and spiky.

He got to his feet and explored it with his hands. A pillarlike shape, almost knee high, smooth, cool, and damp. He walked around it and took another step and then another, his hands out in front of him, trying to move so that the fresh air was blowing directly onto his face.

Something cold and clammy brushed his shoulder. He let out a scared shout and backed away, his heart thumping. His voice echoed to and fro. This place must be *huge.* Finally the echo died and there was silence, except for the faint rhythmic plop of water falling from a height. His outstretched fingers discovered a stony shape that hung, he guessed, from the ceiling far above his head. It ended in a softly rounded point level with his chest.

Any more bits like that, I could knock my brains out, he thought grimly.

But he remembered—and that made all the difference, because he was no longer afraid in the same way—something seen on TV at school. Limestone pillars, hanging curtains, and folds of rock. Stalac-something. *Stalactites and stalagmites*, that was it.

The dark space he was in didn't feel like the Crazy House at the fair any more. He knew it must be a limestone cave, and the odds of there being more than one way into a limestone cave were pretty good. All he had to do was keep going up, paying attention to the direction of the draft and not getting bopped on the head or tripped up by one of these stone pillars if he could help it.

He shuffled forward, one arm out in front of him, the other bent across to protect his face. His ribs hurt furiously, but he was getting almost used to the pain now. The hardest thing was not *staring*. He found he was straining ahead into the blackness, and it was doing odd things to his eyes. At one moment he thought he saw a dancing green phosphorescence, but when he blinked and looked again, it was gone. Once he thought he heard a pebble fall. He stopped and listened, his heart thumping.

"Is anyone there?"

His voice echoed back, high and wobbly. "Anyone there? . . . there?" But there was no other sound.

At last he came to a slope and, beyond it, had to scramble up what felt, to his groping hands, like a set of rough steps leading farther upward.

"Hello?"

The echo came back more quickly. He felt sand and fresh mud under his feet instead of slime. He *must* be close to the exit, if there was one. His heart beat suffocatingly fast. He stared again, but could see nothing. He could no longer feel the draft on his face. There was no indication as to which way he should go.

He turned to his right and shuffled forward until his fingers met a rock face. He followed it around to his left, counterclockwise, feeling upward as high as he could reach for a crack, a step, some indication of the way out.

It took a long time to explore the whole surface, but at last the wall wasn't there any more and his waving hand touched nothing. He took a tentative step forward and his foot met space. He teetered for a terrifying instant on the brink before he got his balance and fell to his knees. He tried to explore whatever was in front of him with his hands. He leaned down and felt a ledge below him. And another, farther down. He realized slowly that he'd come full circle to the stairs he had just climbed. On the one side was the way back down to the lake. On the other three sides a high rock face. There wasn't a way out after all. His escape route was only another dead end.

He crawled across the cave until his back was against the rock wall and sat there, wondering what to do next. He shut his eyes against the terrible blackness, and green lights danced on his closed eyelids. Greenish shapes flickering on and off, like fluorescent arrows.

I'm going crazy, he thought, and screamed out loud, "Get out of my head. Go away!"

The green lights faded away and, in the darkness behind his eyes, he seemed to see Lethbridge. The ravine at sunset, purple shadows against the crimson rock. Dry summer winds and the scent of sage. He could *smell* it. And taste Aunt Gloria's saskatoon pie, dripping with purple berries. And feel the softness of the duvet on his bed, Aunt Gloria's good-night kiss on his forehead.

Walter slept.

He woke from a dream in which he was gliding down the Oldman River in his canoe, the spray from the bow wave on his face, to find himself outside again, lying on his back on the hill, the one he'd been exploring when he fell through the sinkhole. It was raining. Apart from his undershirt and shorts, he was naked. He sat up, shivering, and rubbed his arms and legs, rough with goosebumps. There, straight ahead of him across the marsh, winked the lights of the compound. Below him, a couple of hundred meters away, was the plastic walkway, glimmering in the pale Aqua twilight.

He got stiffly to his feet. How had he got here? Or

was this another tantalizing dream? He *felt* awake. And abominably cold. He was just regretting his rain gear, abandoned on the islet so far underground, when a glimmer of yellow closeby caught his eye. He turned and stared at his clothes, carefully laid out on the ground: the jacket, hood up and arms extended; below it the overpants; and at their feet, his boots. In the deepening twilight it looked like a cartoon picture of a flattened yellow man.

He stared at it numbly and then scrambled thankfully into pants and jacket, his teeth chattering. He was just pulling on his second boot when it suddenly hit him. How had his clothes got here? Laid out that way, as if whoever'd done it had a weird sense of humor. Come to that, how had *he* got here? Who had carried him out of the cave? And why had they left him here instead of taking him back to the compound?

Obviously it had to be someone who was shy and didn't want to be seen. Only who?

He finished pulling on his boot and staggered stiffly down the slope to the walkway. He walked back across the swamp automatically, one foot plodding down in front of the other, his whole body screaming with pain and fatigue. His mind whirled with questions. None of the workers would have left him dumped on the hillside. What about Gordon and his friends? It was the sort of joke a kid would appreciate. But how would they know where he'd gone? He could swear there had been no one behind him on the walkway that morning. Only

Solveig had seen him go. And he distinctly remembered sitting on the hillside eating his lunch, looking back toward the compound, thinking how peaceful it was with not a living soul in sight.

But if it wasn't the grown-ups or the kids, then who could it be? As his mind went over and over these unanswerable questions, he forgot about the damaged plastic. The walkway sank suddenly under his feet, pitching him face forward into the water. It didn't matter getting wet again—he was already wet and cold enough—but the jolt to his side was agony. He crawled out on the far side of the break, got to his knees, and managed to stagger to his feet. His legs were so tired he could hardly keep going. The rain spat down and he wiped his wet hand across his cold face. Once he reached the shore he still had to struggle up the hill to his house. He stopped for breath, his hand to his side.

"Hullo?" A voice came softly out of the mizzle.

He stopped and peered through the gloom. "Solveig?"

"Yeah. Are you all right, Walt?"

He tried to straighten up. "Sure. Why?"

"When you didn't get back for supper your father got kinda worried. He's been asking everyone where you'd got to."

"What did you tell him?"

"Nothing. Was that all right? I thought maybe that's what you'd want."

"Yeah." He wondered vaguely why she was out there,

seemingly waiting for him. Asking himself what on earth he was going to say to his father, he stumbled, one step after another, to the house at the top of the hill and pushed open the door. His father was waiting for him.

"Where the *hell* have you been?" Walt couldn't tell whether it was rage or anxiety that powered the passion in his father's voice.

"Down south. Just exploring." Somehow, though he couldn't say why, it was terribly important that he tell nobody about the caves, the starry lights, or his impossible escape—especially not his father. Not until he'd had time to think it out. He latched onto the only reality that would make sense, that would do as an excuse. "The walkway to the south's broken in two. It just *went.* Knocked me into the water."

The colonel swore again. "There too? Are you all right? You look terrible."

"My ribs. I think they're cracked." Walt managed to kick off his boots and struggle out of his rain pants. The jacket defeated him and his father had to help. He whistled when he saw the bruises on Walt's side, and touched the place with a firm but surprisingly gentle hand. Walt tried to stand up straight and not flinch, not burst into exhausted tears.

"You should get those ribs X-rayed."

"Tomorrow," Walt managed to say. "Bed now."

"Right, son. Okay. You're as cold as a frog. Get under a hot shower and then into bed. I'll put a bandage around your chest and get you some soup."

It felt very peculiar to be sitting in bed, the covers wrapped around him, while the colonel brought him hot soup. Peculiar, but nice. After he'd warmed up a bit he remembered something. "You weren't surprised—about the walkway melting, I mean."

"Been happening all over. Ever since we started cutting the main drainage canal."

"Is there something wrong with the plastic?"

"No, there isn't. It's Aqua that's wrong. It's going to be a brute, this planet. I can feel it in my bones. You meet ones like that once in a while, planets that fight you every centimeter of the way."

"It felt like acid." Walt remembered his stinging fingertips.

"Exactly what it is. We thought it was something released from the soil when we began the big cut. But the scientist joes have narrowed it down to some freakish water snails. Their slime just eats through the plastic. Crazy. How'd the snails know to go for the parts of the walkway smack in between the piers, where the stress is greatest? Smart snails—just what I need!"

"What are you going to do about them?"

"We sure can't kill every snail on Aqua, much as I'd like to. We'll start with an extra protective coating on the walkways, something with a pesticide thrown in. If that acid starts getting into the machinery, we'll be in big trouble." The colonel ran a hand through his short-cropped hair and for a minute looked, Walt thought, like anyone else's father, instead of a hardbitten terraformer. Then he smoothed his hair back and turned toward the door.

"Need a painkiller? Something to help you sleep?" he asked awkwardly.

Walt shook his head. He could hardly keep his eyes open as it was.

"Right then. Take it easy. Report to sick bay first thing in the morning."

The door swung shut behind him, leaving Walt to drain his mug of soup and ponder the impossibilities of Aqua—a planet with no intelligent life forms, where string was twined and knotted, where snails ate through the walkways, where *something* with a weird sense of humor had not only rescued him, but had gone back to the underground island for his rain gear.

I should have told him, his conscience nagged guiltily at him. But he and his father were only just beginning to learn to talk to each other. If he'd told him about the alien "something" that had rescued him, Father would have thought he was nuts. It would be awful. Impossible.

He sighed and put the soup mug down on the bedside table. He slid carefully under the covers, gasping at the tweak of pain in his side. Just before sleep overwhelmed him, he imagined the "something" laughing its fool head off at the sight of him lying on the hillside in his undershorts. And he suddenly remembered that flash among the reeds, gone almost before he had seen it, of a wide green face and slanting amber eyes.

FOUR

On Sunday morning Walt crawled stiffly out of bed and reported to sick bay. Dr. Helgaard X-rayed his chest and frowned over his bruises. "How did you come by these?"

"Fell off a walkway." He decided it would be safer to stick to his story of the previous night.

"Into water? You got these bruises falling into water?"

"Maybe I hit the edge of the walkway," he muttered.

"Or maybe you got beat up. Gordon and his gang?"

"No!" He looked up, startled, to see her eyes looking steadily into his.

"Was it…the colonel?"

He flushed angrily. How could she ask such a question? "My father would never hit me."

"Okay. I beg your pardon. Now, sit here." She strapped his chest from armpits to waist and sent him home to take it easy for the rest of the day.

He felt like a living mummy when he walked stiffly into class on Monday morning.

"So I hear you had a fall on one of the walkways. Bad luck." Ms. Cunningham smiled sympathetically.

Gordon whispered "Earth Looby" just loud enough for everyone to hear, and the boys laughed.

"That's quite enough, Gordon. Settle down, everyone. Time for biology. On Friday I was discussing the anatomy of the amphibian. This morning we will work in pairs dissecting specimens. See if you can identify the various structures I spoke of. I suggest that one of each pair does the dissecting and the other the drawings . . . less messy."

There was a lot of shuffling around and horseplay as the students paired up and picked the best places at the bench under the window. When they'd settled down Walt found himself standing alone in the middle of the room looking at Solveig. *The two outsiders,* he thought.

She twitched her stiff braids back over her shoulder. "Come on then," she said stiffly. "I suppose *you* want to have all the fun and do the dissecting?"

Walt looked at the froglike creature lying on its back on the cutting board. Its arms and legs were widespread, exposing its pale belly. The rest of its skin was a smooth pale green. Though its head was tipped back, exposing the throat, so he couldn't see its face, he felt sure that the eyes would be amber-colored and slanting. The same, only much, much, smaller.

He shuddered, swallowed sudden nausea, and managed to say casually, "That's all right. You go ahead. I'm pretty good at drawing."

"All right!" She beamed at him. When she smiled he couldn't help noticing that her small pale face lit up and she looked okay. She pulled on a pair of plastic gloves, picked up the scalpel, and skillfully slit the belly skin across and down.

"I'll pin the flaps back and you can draw the muscle structure of the abdomen. Then I'll dissect an arm and a leg before we go into the abdomen. Okay by you?"

"Sure." Walt tried to concentrate on his drawing, getting each fold of exposed muscle in the correct place with the fibers running in the right direction, trying not to think of the froglike face among the reeds.

"Your drawing's pretty good."

"So's your dissection."

"I'm going to be a surgeon like Mom when I grow up. But not on missions like this." Her voice sounded scornful. "I'll go to some planet where they need doctors and help make everyone well again. It'll be great. I suppose you'll be a terraformer like your father?"

Though her voice wasn't rude, Walt found himself flushing from his neck right up to his forehead. "No, I won't." His voice rose. "I don't know what I'll be, but it won't be that."

"Shh. You don't have to shout. I'm going to slit the tissue and expose the organs now. Got a fresh piece of paper?"

"Okay." Walt took a deep breath, surprised at the

anger that had suddenly surged through him. He admired his father more than anyone in the galaxy, didn't he? He wanted to be just like him. Didn't he?

As he began to draw the internal organs of the amphibian, he found himself sneaking sideways looks at Solveig. Her tongue was nipped between her teeth and her concentration was total as she probed carefully at the small carcass. Walt found himself envying her singleness of purpose. It must be great to know where you're supposed to be going. What you're supposed to do with your life.

"Your mom fixed my ribs. She's awfully good, isn't she?"

"Yeah. She's kinda neat as a mom too. There when you need her, but she doesn't get in the way, you know."

Walt nodded, though he really didn't. Aunt Gloria had been enormously kind, but she *had* fussed.

"Come on then, wake up." She nudged him. "I'm lifting the liver and heart out of the way. Say, if you want to leave the labeling till we're finished, I can do it for you."

"I'm fine." He felt himself bristling. Not that her voice was actually bossy, but..."I do remember Friday's class."

"Sorry."

They worked on in silence.

"Um...What's that bit behind there?"

"You mean you don't know?" Her eyebrows went up. He flushed and she giggled. "Well, I don't know either. We'll have to ask Ms. Cunningham. Something special to Aqua, I guess. Animals are different all over, you know. Two hearts, two livers. Different breathing apparatus. Things like that. Makes it interesting. If I weren't going to be a doctor, I'd be a comparative biologist. What *were* you doing on Saturday, by the way?" she went on in the same tone of voice, so that for a minute the significance of her question didn't hit him. Then he stared at her guiltily. Why had she asked? She'd never asked him anything before. She couldn't know about his adventure, could she?

"The walkway busted and I cracked my ribs," he said carefully.

"Oh? In that order?"

He felt himself getting hot. "What d'you mean?"

"What were you doing before that? All day. I saw you go, if you remember. I thought it would be fun to go too." She didn't sound accusing, but he felt suddenly mad at her. She had no right making him feel guilty.

"Just exploring." He kept his voice vague, bored-sounding. It was *his* secret, after all.

She shrugged and tossed back a braid that had slipped forward over her shoulder. "Okay. If that's the way you want it." It was as though a light had switched off. Her face wasn't lively and glowing any more. She looked plain and dull. They finished the dissection and the drawings in silence.

As she ripped off her gloves he looked up to find her staring at him. His palms began to sweat. He found himself stammering, "Look, I'm sorry. I didn't mean..."

"No problem." She shrugged.

He managed a light laugh. "I'd like to take you up on that offer of judo lessons."

Her eyebrows went up. "With cracked ribs? Come on!"

Walt stared down at his drawings, struggling with his need to be safe from Gordon's harassing and his need to tell someone his enormous secret.

"I want to tell you about it," he found himself saying. "But not here. Not now."

She glanced past him at Gordon and Li, who were noisily fooling around next to them. She nodded. "Yeah. Okay." She gave him a sudden smile that made the ache in his ribs and the itch of the plaster seem unimportant. For a minute he wanted to jump up and sing. Then he took a deep breath and neatly labeled the last drawing, trying to keep his hand from shaking. What had he gone and done? He couldn't possibly tell her exactly what had happened. She'd think he was crazy. He'd have to make up something to put her off.

He stared down at the neatly dissected frog-creature, its inner mysteries unveiled by Solveig's scientific scalpel. She'd laugh at him. Laugh and tell the others. Either they'd think he'd made up the whole thing and it'd be as bad as the birthday poem, or else maybe they'd believe him and that'd be worse. He couldn't bear the thought of them trampling through the secret caves, shining their floodlights onto the starry roof. What was he to do?

"Look, would you like to come to dinner? Mom won't mind."

"Don't you eat in the cafeteria?"

"Not if I can help it. Mom's a fabulous cook and she likes to keep her hand in. I get to eat her experiments. Even breaded frogs' legs." She began to laugh and then stopped at the expression on his face. "It's not gross, honestly it's not. Better than camp food. Like chicken, really. You're not a vegetarian, are you? It's okay if you are."

He shook his head. "It's not that."

She laughed. "I won't press you. If you really want to eat cafeteria food, go ahead. You could come over after supper, if you like, and we can talk then."

"I don't know if Father..." He stopped at the expression on her face. He couldn't bear to see that light switch off again. He was going to have to risk telling her everything. Maybe she wouldn't laugh. Maybe it would be a good idea. "Okay. After dinner. I'd like that. Thanks."

Walt was in the bathroom, trying to slick his hair into shape, when his father came home.

"What are you up to, boy? All dressed up."

"Just going down to the surgery."

"Your ribs bothering you?"

"No, Father. I'm fine. Dr. Helgaard's daughter, Solveig, is in my class, that's all. She asked me over."

"Go right ahead, son." His father was beaming. Walt

could almost see him thinking: at last my son's stopped writing poetry and is going out with girls. He's *normal*.

Walt hesitated outside the surgery. It was a long building with living quarters at one end. He could hear voices and laughter and he felt like an intruder. But once the door was opened he was drawn effortlessly into the family warmth. They chatted for a while. Solveig mixed up a synthetic fruit drink for them and then turned to her mother.

"I guess you're pretty busy, aren't you, Mom?"

"Yes, I dare say I have some work to catch up on." Her eyes twinkled and she went into the surgery, leaving them together. Walt's mouth fell open. He'd never in a million years dare to dismiss his father in that casual joking way.

Solveig sat down next to Walt and linked her hands around her knees. "Well? Go ahead and tell me what really happened. I'm dying of curiosity."

"It's not that much," he stammered. "Just that I was exploring over on that other hill and I fell down a hole into a cave." He scuffed his feet on the floor.

She laughed. "Walt, you're a terrible liar. You can't have had any practice at all. Come on, I know there's much more to it than that."

"What d'you mean?" He felt his cheeks getting hot.

"You're making it sound like falling into a cave's just nothing. A *cave!* So what is it you're hiding?"

"Nothing really." He stumbled over the words.

"Walter Elliot, listen to me. I'm pretty much on my own here. Because Mom's the doctor it makes her an officer, like your father. Like you, I don't have any friends. It's okay. I'm kind of used to it. But it'd be a lot more fun if we did things together, don't you think?"

"Yes, it would. I'd like that very much."

"Well, then. Friends don't have secrets from each other, and they don't *lie* about things. Right?"

"I suppose..." Walt pulled himself together. "I mean, sure, you're right. I...I'd like to tell you. But it's all so weird. You'll never believe me. Maybe none of it *did* happen. Maybe I just hit my head and imagined everything."

"Like what?" She was on to him like a dog on a gopher.

"Kinda like lights," he muttered feebly. "In the cave."

"Lights?" Her eyes looked at him the way Doctor Helgaard's had, scientific and yet kind at the same time. "Were they natural, do you suppose?"

"I don't know."

"You do, though, don't you? Come on, Walt, tell me. No, better than that, *show* me. Wow, imagine exploring a cave unknown to all other humans! Please, Walt. It'd be such fun, and Aqua's so *boring*."

"Well, I suppose..." He felt himself giving way weakly to the pleading in her hazel eyes. But to go back into that darkness. . .

"Promise?" she shot back, her eyes suddenly snapping.

When he nodded she gave him another beaming smile. He felt suddenly that he'd been had, that somehow she'd got him to precisely this point of not being able to back out. Then he wondered if she could read his mind, because she started laughing. It was so infectious that he found himself reluctantly joining in, all the time wondering: *What am I doing?*

"It'll be all right, Walt. You can trust me, truly you can. And maybe two heads will be better than one."

He stared. "What for?"

"For thinking with, dummy. If the lights aren't a natural phenomenon, if there really *is* an intelligent species on Aqua, then we have no right to be here, have we?"

It was the way she was with the scalpel, he thought—direct and cutting, with no wasted motions. She was already way ahead of him, prepared to accept the possibility of intelligent beings on Aqua.

"Yes, of course. That's the problem exactly. Only...there can't really be intelligent beings here, can there? It stands to reason."

"That's what we're going to have to find out. Then we can decide what we're going to do about it, right?"

He frowned. He was beginning to dislike her habit of backing him into a corner and jumping to conclusions. "I'm just going to show you a *cave,* Solveig."

"I know. But I'm sure it's linked with the mysterious lights. And maybe with the dissolving walkways and the snails. This is exciting! There's more to Aqua than meets the eye, Walt Elliot."

He had the feeling that she was right. Again.

■ ■ ■

The snails went on multiplying. By now all the walkways had collapsed, and the tractor treads were being attacked. The whole area to the north of the compound hill, where the work of digging drains and erecting dikes was going on, was infested with snails, their silvery trails beginning to eat into everything that wasn't part of Aqua.

Walt could see his father's dream collapsing around him. "What'll you do?" he asked one evening.

The colonel's temper suddenly flared. He swore and threw his glass across the room. "A few liters of systemic poison in the groundwater and I could take care of the whole problem."

Walt turned from picking up the glass—it was plastic, of course, so no damage had been done—and froze. *Poison the water?* He thought of the green face with its amber eyes. Oh, no!

"But those bleeding-heart do-gooders back at Federation Headquarters with their tom-fool rules won't allow it. How'm I supposed to get the job done with my hands tied behind my back?"

Walt breathed again and put the glass on the table.

The colonel's solution was almost as horrible as poison. He had all the snails dredged up, dumped in a shining pile, and lasered to a sticky goo. The remains stank. The smell of burning snail shells hung over the compound and got into everyone's hair and clothes, like the bitter tang of a forest fire. Even the food tasted of it. Tempers began to fray and Walt heard ugly words about the colonel, stories about what he'd done on other planets. He tried to shut his ears to the mutterings and lie low, to be as invisible as possible. He even tried to avoid Solveig, but she'd have none of that.

"Hey, it's a disgusting solution, but it's not your fault, Walt. Lighten up!"

By the end of a week it seemed that the problem was licked, and his father became almost jovial, sitting with Walt on the porch, quaffing a beer. "The secret of success is never giving way, son. Never even imagining the possibility of failure. I know I can beat Aqua, the way I've beaten other planets. Every one…since Saturnis Five." When his jaw clamped tight, so his face looked like a stone statue, Walt knew he was thinking about his dead mother.

He wanted desperately to say something that would help, but he couldn't think of anything. He put his hand on his father's arm. The colonel looked at him. "You're more like her every day." He put his hand over Walt's and they sat on the porch, listening to the rain.

The next week another generation of snails hatched and the whole horrible business of lasering them to extinction was gone through again. On the Saturday after Dr. Helgaard had taken the strapping off Walt's cracked ribs, he and Solveig were sitting on the surgery porch. The stench of burning snails drifted up on the wet breeze. It was sickening.

"I'm sure glad your ribs have healed at last. I can't

wait to get away from the camp. Think you'll be fit enough to go back to the cave tomorrow?"

"I guess so. Yes, it'll be good to get away. The only problem is that the walkway to the other hill's dissolved, and I heard Father say they're not going to bother replacing it. All the work's being done up in the north. There's nothing down south to make it worth their while."

"Well, that's good in a way, isn't it? It means nobody'll interfere with us. Is the marsh shallow enough for us to wade through?"

"I doubt it. And it would take us for ever. Have you ever tried to walk through even knee-high water? But there are some small boats the survey crews use."

"Could you ask your father if we could borrow one?"

"He's in a foul mood these days, Solveig. Those snails..."

"Are you trying to wriggle out of your promise, Walter Elliot?"

"No. Course not. But I don't think I'll ask him for a boat. If he said no we'd be stuck. Let's just borrow one."

"There's my boy." Solveig grinned at him. "How'll we do it?"

"I thought that if I slipped out of the house before Father was up tomorrow, I could sneak down to the boathouse, get a canoe or something, and paddle away from the work site before the morning shift goes on."

"And what about me?"

"I could pick you up south of the compound."

"Leaving you to have all the fun? No way! I'll meet you outside your house before daylight. What time?"

"Father's usually up at six. Can you manage five o'clock?"

"Sure. I'll tell Mom I'll be away for the day so she won't worry. How about you? What'll you tell your dad?"

"He doesn't usually worry about what I'm doing on weekends, but to be on the safe side I'll leave my bed so it looks like I'm still sleeping. Then he won't bother me. And he won't be back till after supper, if then. The only thing I'm not sure of is waking up on time. I can't use an alarm clock. He'd hear it for sure."

"I'll scratch on your window. Leave it open a bit and I'll throw stones at you if you don't wake up right away. And I'll get us lunches from the cafeteria."

Solveig's eyes sparkled and Walt wondered again what he'd got himself into. She was a bit like a runaway horse, galloping off with him farther than he'd dare go on his own. And he didn't know how to rein her in. "But...," he began to protest.

"But nothing." She smiled at him. "You need a friend, Walter Elliot. And, like I said, two heads are better than one."

She was right, of course. That was the trouble: she nearly always was. "Okay. You be there at five."

It went like clockwork. Walt woke at the first tap against his window and peered out. Solveig was crouching on the ground directly below. Quickly he pulled on his clothes and rain gear, cramming his flashlight into the pocket. He rolled up his blanket and flopped it onto the bed in as realistic a pose as he could, and covered it with his sheet. Then he pushed the window fully open and slid through, closing it carefully behind him.

They ran silently down the hill, past the houses, the school, and the cafeteria. Past the work site where the great earth-movers stood like sleeping dinosaurs, while workers swarmed over them, repairing the damage caused by the snails. They slipped through the shadows to the row of supply huts. The doors weren't locked; there was no place on Aqua to hide any stolen goods, so there were no thieves and no need of locks. Close to the water, in the last hut, were the boats, small plastic canoes. They hadn't been used since the initial survey, Walt guessed, and so hadn't been attacked by the snails.

"There's no engine. How does it go?"

Walt stared. "Arm power, of course." He pointed to the paddles clipped to the thwarts. "Haven't you ever seen a canoe?"

"Uh-uh. Do you know how to make it go?"

"I grew up paddling on the Oldman River. Compared with that, this place is like a bathtub. Come on. Lift up that end."

"Okay." Her voice was nervous, as if she were having second thoughts.

"The reeds'll be a nuisance. You'll have to help me by paddling a bit from the bow, so we don't get tangled. Climb in then."

"You're sure it won't sink?"

"Of course not. Get in. Unless you'd rather not go." It felt good being the one in charge, for a change.

"Huh!" Solveig bounced into the boat and it grounded on the boggy bottom. Walt had to heave the stern free and jump for it. The boat wobbled and righted itself as he knelt, his back against the crossbar, his fingers already crooked around the paddle, feeling the familiar tug against the water.

"What do I do now? What am I supposed to do?" Solveig's voice rose.

"Ssh. Don't yell. Someone'll hear. Sound carries like crazy over water. Hold your paddle like this, your left hand snugged over the top, right hand circling it loosely, partway down. Keep it on the right side of the bow and push in toward the boat to turn us to the right, and outward to turn us left. If there's a real tangle dead ahead, tell me whether to aim left or right."

"Like this? Is this okay?"

"That's fine, Solveig. But don't worry anyway. I can paddle single-handed if I have to. It's just easier with someone in the bow, especially with all these reeds."

It felt good to be back in a familiar element. The paddle fit comfortably in his hand and he knelt tall, seeing, past Solveig's neat head, the silvery grayness of small patches of open water between clumps of reeds and seemingly impenetrable carpets of quaggy moss. It felt good to feel again the pressure of water against his paddle, to hear the faint splash as he drew it out and dug in again.

"D'you suppose anyone can see us?" Solveig whispered.

"Not a chance, even if they were looking this way. The reeds are way over our heads."

Down here, against the water, was the real Aqua, Walt found himself thinking. Not like the compound, where every scrap of vegetation had been scraped away and replaced with walks, houses, and workshops. Not like the work site, where the earth-movers gouged into the mud. Down here was the real planet, gray in the predawn light, untouched by human technology.

This made Walt think about the snails. Their numbers were declining, he knew, after a third burn-off. Was the canoe safe? He couldn't imagine anything as slow as a snail catching up and attaching itself to the bottom of the boat and eating it away, but he reminded himself that they'd be wise to haul it right out of the water and inspect its bottom once they reached the southern hill. Just in case.

The sun rose on their left, a pale smudge behind the gray cloud cover, and the sky lightened slowly, coloring the reeds and the water. Now that the excavators had been grounded, it was breathlessly quiet, the only sound the faint gurgle of their paddles and the plink of droplets falling back into the water. The reeds whispered by, close on either side, and golden pollen drifted onto their hair and shoulders.

"It's so beautiful," Solveig whispered. "To think I've been on Aqua all this time and never knew it was like this."

Over to their left, toward the pale blur of sun, Walt saw a silver gleam and forced the canoe between the reeds toward it. It was one of the main streams that came down from the other hill and meandered across the marsh between. Now they could make much better headway, and in a little over a couple of hours they beached the canoe on solid ground, some fifteen kilometers or so away from the base camp.

Solveig jumped out and lifted her bag from the bottom of the canoe. "I don't know about you, but I'm *starving*. I brought enough for breakfast as well as lunch, so let's dig in."

After Walt had hauled the canoe ashore and tipped it over to make sure no snails had attached themselves to its bottom, they ate breakfast and set off up the hill. It was turning into what passed for a fine day on Aqua: a faint drizzle that just prickled their skin and filmed their hair with fine drops. There was no wind. They were both wearing rubber-soled shoes, much easier for tramping through the bush in than the high rainboots Walt had worn before.

Now that he knew it was there, Walt found the sinkhole with no difficulty at all. Solveig knelt at its edge, pulling aside the vegetation that masked it, and dropped a pebble. They counted to three before they heard it bounce and scutter among the stones on the tiny islet below.

"I don't know why you weren't *killed*." She backed away from the edge, her face suddenly white. "So where's the hole you escaped through?"

Was this the moment to tell Solveig about the mysterious someone who had rescued him? Walt rubbed his nose and evaded the question. "I don't know. It was pitch-dark in there. But it should be more or less in a straight line with the place where that stream begins, where I tried to get out first, and the sinkhole."

"Close by?"

He shook his head. "I wandered around in the dark for ages, maybe as much as a kilometer, maybe only half that. I'm not really sure."

He saw her eyes on him, questioning. "You do believe me, don't you?"

"I don't see how you *ever* found your way out. You didn't even have a flashlight, did you?"

Walt shook his head, feeling his cheeks grow hot. How was he ever going to tell her the really crazy part of his adventure? She'd never believe him in a million years.

She went on, as if she hadn't noticed his embarrassment. "If we can mark the spring and the sinkhole with something and keep them one behind the other as we search, we'll stay on a more or less straight line. That way we ought to find the exit."

"If it really *is* on a straight line. I wish I'd thought of bringing some survey tape." He looked thoughtfully at Solveig's braids, which were tied with bright yellow ribbons. "Those ribbons of yours would show up for quite a distance, wouldn't they?"

Solveig sighed and pulled the ribbons off. "Here you are. In the interest of science."

The stream bubbled out of a tiny cleft in the rock. He'd been crazy to imagine he could have got out that way, Walt thought. Nothing larger than a minnow or a tadpole could get through. Solveig tied one ribbon high in a bush overhanging the spring, and the second onto the branch of a lush broad-leaved creeper sprawling over the edge of the sinkhole.

The two ribbons fluttered gaily in the breeze. There was a scent of fresh herbs in the air, clean and medicinal after the sickening stench of burning snails. *In spite of the drizzle and the gray sky, Aqua isn't at all bad,* Walt thought as they climbed the hill, hunting to either side for a cleft in the rock that might hide an opening to the cave beneath. They looked back now and then to check that the marker ribbons were still roughly one above the other.

The slope became more rugged, and ledges of rock stuck out like ribs from the ground cover. It was under one of these ledges that Walt found the footprint. It had been made in damp dirt and the edges were blurred, but it was still unmistakably a footprint.

The foot splayed out in a wide triangle. It had only four digits. "So it can't be human, can it?" said Solveig, spreading out her hand beside it, her fingers spanning the print almost exactly. Looking down at it and at Solveig's hand alongside, Walt remembered the biology lab and tried to imagine a Solveig-sized frog. Yellow eyes and a wide forehead...it still seemed impossible, even with the evidence of this print. An alien being. Something out of a video.

He shook his head. "Maybe it's a joke. Maybe Gordon and the others, trying to get a rise out of us..." His voice faded.

"Not those guys. They haven't the imagination."

"But it *is* human size. Small human. How could the survey team have missed something this big?"

"There must be very few of them," she suggested. "Or else they're very shy."

"That makes sense. Like giant pandas. Or orangutans." Solveig looked puzzled. "Earth animals," he went on. "There were travelers' stories about them for years, and finally they were discovered and put in zoos. They're extinct now."

She sighed and then said practically, "Let's eat our lunch. Less to carry."

They ate, looking across the marsh to the work site on the far side of the other hill. One of the dinosaur diggers, the size of an ant from here, was at work again, gouging black channels into the soil. Obviously the colonel was on his way to conquering the snails.

"I just wish..."

"Me too." Solveig leaned back and stretched. "Ow!"

"What's the matter?"

"I almost fell. There wasn't anything there—oh, Walt, look!" She pulled the creepers aside. Behind the hanging vegetation was an oblong of shadow, wide enough to creep into. "Hey, I think we've found it!"

FIVE

"It's your cave, Walt. You go first."

"If it's the right one. We don't know that for sure yet." He wriggled cautiously through the opening and slipped on the wet floor inside. "Look out!" He gave a hand to Solveig and waved his flashlight around. The cave was disappointingly small, little more than a swelling in a passage that vanished into darkness. Even when he shone the light directly at the dark patch he could see only rock walls and more shadow. It had to be the way in, if this was the right place, but it looked awfully narrow. Suppose they started exploring and got stuck? He hesitated.

"Does that passage go on for long?" He could feel Solveig's breath warm against his cheek.

"I don't know. I still don't know if it's the right cave."

"But you must remember."

"I guess I'm going to have to tell you. But you'll never believe me." Walt reluctantly explained about seeing the mysterious lights and then falling asleep. "I know it sounds nuts, but that's what happened. I knew I was trapped. Then I went to sleep and had some weird dreams. When I woke up I was out there."

"'On the cold hill's side,'" Solveig quoted. "Like the poor knight in *La Belle Dame Sans Merci*. Maybe this is a magic cave. Who knows what'll happen to us? We might come out a hundred years later, or be turned into pigs."

Solveig sounded thrilled with the idea, and Walt chuckled; it was neat knowing someone who'd read the same books. Suddenly the weight of fear slipped from his shoulders. "Let's go on and see what happens, then."

The passage was low as well as narrow, and he dropped to his knees. Painful though this was, it seemed safer to shuffle along, ready for any surprises. After a while the passage turned toward the left. When he shone the flashlight in front of him, the light danced in small gold circles on damp rock directly ahead.

"You all right?" His voice boomed unexpectedly, as if he were talking into a jug.

"Just fine." Solveig sounded cheerful, not fussing a bit at the darkness and the damp. *A great person to share an adventure with, to have as a friend,* Walt thought.

The passage turned right and now, when he waved the flashlight around, he was dazzled by color. Solveig bumped into him from behind. "What's the matter?"

"We're there. We've found it."

They had emerged onto a wide, high platform ending abruptly in a drop of some two or three meters. From their vantage point they looked down onto a glittering forest of stone trees. Stone draperies covered the walls. Pillars rose from the floor and hung from the ceiling, all of it sparkling like diamonds as Walt's flashlight darted from detail to detail. It was like being in the choir loft of a cathedral.

"It's the most gorgeous thing I've ever seen. Who built it?"

"Nobody. Nature. It happens on Earth too." For only the second time since arriving on Aqua, Walt felt he knew more about something than everyone else. "Dissolved minerals precipitate out of the ground water. The ones up there are called stalactites and—"

"I don't care about the *names*." He felt a twinge of annoyance at her interruption, until he saw her face shining as she stared around. "It's so…so…"

"Yeah, it is, isn't it?" His annoyance vanished at her excitement.

"How ever did you find your way through those stone pillars without a flashlight?"

He could laugh, now that the nightmare was behind him. With a flashlight and a friend he could conquer the world. "I got *this* far before I gave up." He pointed down to the bottom of the ledge they were standing on. "It's not that high, really. Only just beyond my reach. But in the dark I couldn't see. I thought it was the end of the cave."

"Want to let me down, Walt? Then you can climb down on my back."

They managed the drop with no trouble and picked their way down a staircase of rocky ledges that brought them to a gentle slope and on to a deeper chamber, larger and higher than the first.

"Walt, wait." Solveig stooped to finger the edge of rock. "I know you said the cave happened naturally, but look at this mark. And this. I don't think these stairs happened by themselves."

Walt rubbed his finger over the marks. They were waterworn, but they did remind him of something he'd seen back home on the prairie. Arrowheads, that was it. Stones chipped by other stones, held in a human grasp.

Solveig spread out her hand. "Remember the print outside the cave?"

"Yeah." It felt suddenly spooky. Walt waved the flashlight around and the shadows of the pillars jumped from wall to wall like skinny ghosts. Anything could be down here in the darkness, watching them, and they would never know.

For a second, panic jolted like an electric shock through his body. Then it was gone, and when Solveig shivered he put an arm awkwardly over her shoulder. "It's okay. If they are here, I know they're friendly." He felt so sure, it was as if someone had planted the idea in his head.

He felt her relax. "I know. I feel safe all of a sudden. Let's go on."

He took her hand, warm and surprisingly small in his, and led her down past the last of the pillars and stone draperies to the place where the water lapped, black as ink, against the shore. He kept the light down toward the ground as they walked, and now he switched it off.

"Oh! What's the matter? Is the battery gone? How'll we get back in the dark?"

"Sorry, I didn't mean to scare you." He held her hand tightly. "It's okay. You'll see. Just wait," he whispered.

He pulled her down until they were sitting at the edge of the lake. Slowly, shyly, the lights began to appear, shimmering, dancing on the surface of the water. He looked up. They seemed even more beautiful today, now that he wasn't alone and wasn't afraid. They encrusted the vaulted roof, pulsing with a cold phosphorescent light. He hoped that she wouldn't spoil it by talking, asking questions.

It was all right. Though he couldn't see her, he could sense her stillness beside him. The silence brought a wonderful sense of peace. Walt felt as if he had been drawn out of his body, that somehow he was hovering, weightless, above the dark lake. Into his mind flashed a myriad of bright images, like a wordless story told only in pictures. Time passed, though he had no idea how long; but, at last, the final picture faded and he once again felt the stony ground under his butt, and Solveig's hand warm in his.

She stirred and stretched. Without a word they got

to their feet and turned away from the starry lake. Silently, the flashlight guiding them, they retraced their steps. At the final ledge Walt dropped to his knees so Solveig could climb onto his shoulder. Once safely up, she wriggled around and held out her hands, small but strong, and gave him the necessary lift.

Beyond the twisting entrance tunnel lay the oblong gray of Aqua. It was a lot darker than when they had gone in. "Almost twilight. We'll never make it in time for supper."

"That's all right. Mom'll give us a snack."

"So long as no one asks questions about where we've been."

"Don't worry so." She laughed. "You *are* a worrier, you know, Walt."

He realized that she was right. He'd always worried. About making Aunt Gloria happy. About doing well in school. About his music. And making his father proud of him...How pretty Solveig looked with her fair hair rippling around her face, he suddenly noticed. She should always wear it loose instead of skinned back into those tight braids.

She flushed at his stare and put her hands to her head. "I'm a mess. Oh, my ribbons! We'd better reclaim them before we go."

"They're just ribbons, and we're awfully late already."

"They point to the entrance. *We* found it. So might anyone else."

"Of course. Sorry."

But the ribbons were gone.

"The wind, do you think?"

"I don't see how. I tied them in double knots."

"It's crazy, but at least no one else can use them to find the cave," Walt panted as they jogged down the slope to where they'd left the canoe. He flipped it over and was about to push it back into the water when Solveig stopped him.

"Look!" She began to laugh.

Attached to the center thwarts of the canoe were the yellow ribbons, twisted into a design like the one Walt had tripped over on the walkway weeks before.

"What can it mean?" Solveig wondered.

"Does it have to mean anything? Except that whoever did it has a great sense of humor."

"I think so." She fingered the crossed and twisted strands. "Of course I don't really know, but I *think* it means something like 'hello.'"

Walt paddled as fast as his newly healed ribs would let him. The canoe glided smoothly, as if it were finding its own way home, the silvery thread of clear water unwinding ahead of him. Solveig had quickly got the knack of the best way to paddle from the bow, and her muscle power gave him the extra headway to steer effectively. It was still not quite dark when they beached the canoe and hauled it back to the boat shed.

As he closed the shed door, Walt hesitated. Part of

him wanted to tell Solveig about the weird thing that had happened to him when they were sitting by the lake looking at the lights, but the cautious part of him—the old Walt—wanted to keep it to himself, to mull it over secretly and decide what it meant. While he was still hesitating, looking up the hill, she grabbed his hand. "Come on. I'll get us something to eat at home. We've got to talk about what happened down at the lake."

Dr. Helgaard was out. Solveig vanished and came back in a red jumpsuit with her hair neatly rebraided. She tossed him a terrycloth robe. "Get out of your things and warm up." She vanished again, and, when he had skinned off his rain gear, he followed her into the doctor's surgery. Solveig had the refrigerator door open and was browsing among sinister-looking tubes and specimen jars. She came out with a jar of a dark red substance.

"What on earth is *that*?"

She laughed at his expression. "Spaghetti sauce. Fill that pan with hot water, will you?" She lit a burner.

Fifteen minutes later they were sitting on cushions on the living-room floor with big bowls of spaghetti.

"Well?" Solveig challenged him. "Do you want to talk first, or shall I?"

Walt hesitated. The ideas that had filled his head in the cave were so incredible she'd just laugh. Like his poetry. He'd lost Father's respect because of poetry. He didn't want to lose the only friend he had on Aqua.

"That's okay. I'll start." She waved her fork around.

"I wish I knew how to describe what happened to me. Words don't seem to work. But I was being told—kind of inside my head—all sorts of things about Aqua. Afterward, when we came out of the cave, it was like I was seeing Aqua through *his* eyes. On the way back, I knew every twist of the river. Like someone else was in my head, sharing his thoughts with me."

The relief was overwhelming. "That's exactly what happened to me, only I was scared to tell you. I thought you'd think I was nuts."

"Like I said, Walt, you worry too much. Anyway, Greenie..."

"Greenie?"

"Well, he had a name, but I couldn't make sense of it."

"Okay. Go on, Solveig."

"He told me about his people. This sounds crazy, but if I understood him, the lights on the cave ceiling are like embryos. Does that make any sense to you? It sure sounds weird to me."

"I thought they were the larval stage of something that changes into something quite different. Like butterflies, you know."

"Why butterflies?"

"Because they start out as eggs that hatch into wormy things. Then later their bodies change into insects with beautiful wings."

"I remember. I've seen pictures. Metamorphosis. That makes sense, because Greenie said the shining things remain in the cave until a special time when the water rises so high it fills the cave to the ceiling. Then they swim away and turn into creatures like..." Her voice suddenly wobbled. "Like the frogs we dissected in class."

"Not really like them." Walt tried to reassure her, though he didn't feel too certain himself. How *did* the Federation decide what made a species "intelligent" anyway? Back home it hadn't seemed to matter. Or had it? There were whales and...

"On Earth there's monkeys and chimps and gorillas. And then there's humans. Our DNA is *that* close to chimps and gorillas." He held up his hand, finger and thumb almost touching. "But humans are still different."

"An opposing thumb? Is that all the difference, Walt?"

"Does it matter?"

"I think so. I think it's going to matter enormously."

Walt rubbed his nose. "Well, humans have a past and a future. The other primates only have the present."

"You mean we've got history?"

"Yeah. And myth."

"And dreams of the future, of course."

"And different ways of looking at ourselves and the world around us. Like with music, art, story."

"Those frog creatures don't have any of that. They can't, can they? They don't have possessions at all, do they?"

"I don't think so. I thought about that when I first arrived on Aqua. When I saw..." Walt stopped.

"Go on."

"I saw one of them. In the reeds. An alien, about the size of the one that made that footprint, I guess."

"And you never told me. Anyway, they're not the aliens. *We* are." Her face flushed.

"Don't get mad at me, Solveig. I didn't tell anyone because, well, it sounded so unbelievable."

"That's okay. Anyway, you were talking about them not having possessions and you said..."

"If you think about it, they can't actually own much, not with the planet flooding every so often. I wish I understood that bit better. I got the feeling that it's something huge and scary, but it's what they're waiting for, because it's their real birth—like caterpillars becoming butterflies. Of course, that's just what humans think. I mean, caterpillars can't think about it, can they? Or butterflies either, come to that."

"But frog people *do* communicate, Walt. Greenie managed to put all those facts in our heads, so it stands to reason they can telepathize with each other—probably as clearly as us talking. Then there's the twined ribbon. Like a cat's cradle, isn't it? A way of telling a story or leaving a message. They may not have books, but I'm sure they have *stories*."

Walt mopped up the last of his sauce with a piece of bread. "So we know two things that prove they're intelligent."

Solveig began to laugh. "Three, actually. They have a sense of humor, that's for sure. Think of them using my ribbons to leave a message!"

"And the way my rain gear was laid out beside me on the hill. But I'd really like to know what they've got to laugh about. If we've got it right, there's going to be something like a tidal wave that washes right over Aqua. When it's gone everything's changed and they have to start all over again. That doesn't sound like fun."

"A *tidal* wave? Is that what the rising water's called? I couldn't figure that bit out. I come from Kwatar, and that's a desert planet."

"On Earth they usually happen after an undersea earthquake. There's some major shift and the sea starts moving. The wave travels real fast, maybe eight hundred kilometers an hour, and grows up to twenty meters high. When it reaches the shore it just piles up and rushes inland..." Walt's voice dried up and he could feel the blood draining out of his face. That was what Greenie had been trying to tell them. That it was going to happen to Aqua. Soon.

"Don't you see, Solveig? A tidal wave would be bound to destroy our whole settlement. It'd drown us all. We'll have to tell our parents..."

Solveig's voice broke into his frightening picture of the compound under meters of raging water. "Walt, are you listening? I said there *is* no earthquake activity on Aqua."

"Are you sure?"

"Of course. Oh, I guess we took that in class before you got here. Ms. Cunningham said there was no seismic activity anywhere on Aqua."

They stared at each other.

"Maybe it's just a myth," Walt suggested. "Or an ancient memory, like the Flood. Or maybe it's not due to happen for hundreds of years..." His voice trailed off uncertainly. It hadn't *felt* unreal, or like something in history or a long way off in the future.

Solveig shook her head. "I don't think so. Greenie sounded kind of happy, like he'd been waiting for whatever it is for a long time, but wasn't going to have to wait much longer. Maybe it's a flood that's got nothing to do with earthquakes."

"What are we going to do?"

"You'll just have to tell your father. If there's really going to be a flood—a tidal wave, whatever—we'll have to leave Aqua."

"Leave Aqua?" Walt gave a hysterical laugh. "If I went to him with a story about a human-size telepathic *frog*, he'd...he'd laser out my brain."

"Don't exaggerate! He can't be that tough."

"He is. Look." Walt hesitated. "Remember how ruthless he was with the snails? I know he's my father, but that doesn't mean he trusts me. Not yet. He—he brought me to Aqua just because I wrote him a poem."

"A poem. Really? Was it *very* rude?"

"Of course not. It was for his birthday. But he was absolutely furious and said Aunt Gloria was ruining me. Can you imagine him believing me if I told him about Greenie?"

"Hmm." Solveig got up and began to prowl around

the room. "The problem is, we don't have enough evidence. Ideas coming at us from those lights in the cave are all very well, but who's going to believe us? You're right. What we've got to do is set up a meeting with Greenie, face to face."

"Hey, wait a minute! You mean, talk to an *alien*?" She was going too fast for him, like a roller-coaster ride. He felt breathless and—he had to admit it—scared. The good feeling that had wrapped warmly around him in the cave had vanished. Now all he could think of were those alien eyes, staring at him through the reeds.

"I told you before, Walter Elliot. *We're* the aliens here. Anyway, what are you afraid of? There's dozens of perfectly friendly nonhuman species out in the galaxy."

"Not in Lethbridge, Alberta, there aren't. And I wish you'd quit being so bossy. I saw them first, and *I* found the cave."

They glared at each other, until Walt broke the silence with a muttered "Sorry."

Solveig sighed. "No, it's my fault. I know I'm bossy. Mom's always telling me. And I keep forgetting you're from Earth. I guess the idea of other intelligent species *is* kind of spooky, if you're only used to humans. Look, go ahead and say what you think we ought to do."

Suppressing the obvious idea of saying nothing to anybody and pretending nothing had happened, Walt racked his brains for a scheme brilliant enough to impress her.

She sat silently, chewing thoughtfully at the end of her braid. Walt found himself staring, and she blushed.

"Sorry. Mom says it's a disgusting habit. I've nearly broken myself of it, honest."

"Huh? No, I was thinking of your ribbons. You're dead right. We've got to find a way to contact Greenie. Suppose we took the canoe out and tied your ribbons among the reeds out on the marsh. Do you think Greenie'd get the idea?"

"That's fantastic!"

"I dunno about that," he said modestly, rather pleased with it himself. Outside, the rain teemed down and he found himself imagining a great wave racing around the planet. "I wonder how long we've got."

"How long?"

"Before the tsunami—the tidal wave—or whatever it is."

"Is it all right if I borrow one of the canoes, Father?" Walt asked on Monday after school, trying to keep his voice casual. His heart thumped loudly in his chest and he had the feeling his father could hear it.

"What for?"

"Oh…exercise mostly. I used to do a lot of canoeing back home. And, well, I thought it might be fun to take Solveig out."

The colonel beamed and Walt felt swamped with guilt. Father was so easy to fool. Walt could read his mind: exercise *and* taking a girl out just proved to his father that he'd made the right choice, taking him away from Aunt Gloria's influence and bringing him to Aqua.

"I'll give you a note. If anyone asks about it you can just show it."

"Thanks, Father," he managed to say, ashamed and yet relieved at how easy it was. Now they could take a canoe any time they wanted without having to sneak around.

The colonel's hand clamped on his shoulder. "Glad you're settling in at last," he said.

"So it's all right," he told Solveig. "We can take a canoe whenever we want to. But I shouldn't have deceived him like that."

"It's not a crime. We're just going out in a canoe, after all."

"But—"

"Walt, you *know* you were right. We can't tell the grown-ups till we figure out what's going on ourselves. Smarten up. Imagine what your dad would have said if you'd asked him for the loan of a canoe to set up a meeting with a giant frog?"

They chose as a meeting place a spot where the stream doubled back on itself to form almost an island. It was out of sight of the compound hill, except for the very top, where the colonel's house stood, but was still only fifteen minutes' paddling time from the boathouse. Here Solveig wove a cat's cradle on her fingers with her spare hair ribbons and cleverly fastened it between two reeds a double handspan apart.

"What'll we do now?" Walt asked. "How will Greenie know what we want?"

"He won't, of course. I think they use cat's cradles to leave messages for each other, maybe when they're too far away for telepathy to work, but we can't even guess what a particular pattern means. But I bet if we come here every day at the same time..."

And it worked. The very next day they came to the same spot and there was Greenie, squatting on the tufts of moss that made up the islet. Walt shuddered and for an awful moment thought he might get sick. Greenie was so very large, so very slimy. So...alien. He swallowed and clenched his fists so that the nails bit into the palms of his hands.

A large frog, Solveig had joked, and Greenie really did look like that. A large talking frog. Walt pinched himself and wished it were all a crazy dream.

Solveig seemed to be taking it perfectly calmly, but of course it was easy for her. She'd been on several weird planets already, and back in *her* home there wasn't any creature like a frog to get in the way of her believing that this large slimy green thing could possibly be an intelligent being.

"Solveig," she said firmly and pointed at herself. "Walt," and she pointed at him. Then she looked questioningly at the amphibian.

He—if it was a he—made an incomprehensible gurgle in his throat. If that was his name, they were not much further ahead. *This really is an alien,* Walt thought. *We have absolutely nothing in common.* He suddenly wondered what Aunt Gloria would have made of it.

The creature squatted on a pad of marsh moss, its head at about the same level as theirs as they sat in the canoe. It was a wide head with well-marked cheekbones, a flat nose, and slanted amber eyes. The pupils were slit horizontally, like those of a horse, which made its face look even wider—as did its mouth, which spread in what seemed to be a humorous grin.

Like dolphins back home on Earth, Walt thought. In marine parks and aquariums they always seemed to be enjoying themselves as they jumped through hoops and returned beach balls to their trainer. But really it was just the set of their mouths, with that little fold in the corner that signals to humans, "I'm happy." Only maybe they weren't.

Certainly this creature had nothing to grin about, if indeed it understood what the invaders from space were going to do to its planet. Walt stopped being quite so frightened and began worrying instead.

Greenie suddenly spoke again. Its voice wasn't at all like a frog's croak, though its throat swelled up like a frog's as the sounds came out. It was deeper, more sonorous, and the sounds had a shape to them. It was definitely language.

"We need your help," Walt said slowly. "We don't understand what you told us in the cave."

"Ah!" Greenie stretched out his long arms and put a

hand lightly on each of their heads. The hands had three fingers and a thumb, Walt had time to notice, trying not to flinch at the touch. The fingers were long and supple, splayed at the tips, and they felt cool and a bit clammy.

Once the hand touched his head, Walt didn't have time to worry about Greenie's appearance, because his head was filled with a rush of ideas, almost as if someone had switched on a radio. It was a bit like listening to a person talking very fast—you got the idea behind what was said rather than the actual words. Walt understood that if he thought what *he* wanted to say, Greenie would understand, but he felt more comfortable putting his thoughts into words. So, evidently, did Solveig.

"Something important's going to happen to Aqua—to your planet, isn't it?" she asked.

Greenie's amber eyes glowed. "Soon." He sounded happy.

"But what is it? In the cave—the pictures in our heads—it looked like a tidal wave. How will it happen? Why?" Walt asked in turn.

"It will be the completion." They both understood, when he spoke these words, that for Greenie the "completion" was the most wonderful thing in the world, something he and his brothers and sisters had waited for all their lives.

"Does that mean that if the wave doesn't come, you won't be complete? Something will be missing?"

Worse than that, it seemed. If the wave didn't cover

Aqua, then the new babies, now glowing lights on the roof of the cave, would dry up and wither away, and that would be the end of intelligent life on Aqua.

"But the wave *will* come." Greenie nodded and his mouth widened reassuringly.

"How often does it come? How long does it stay?"

That was even more difficult to understand. Greenie took Solveig's ribbon and, after admiring its construction, sliding it through his bony fingers, he shook it free and began to loop it into another design, using his splay-tipped fingers and his toes.

They stared at it, trying to puzzle out what it might mean.

"It's a bit like a comet with a long tail," Solveig suggested.

"Or maybe a planet with only part of its orbit shown."

"Is that it, Greenie? Another planet?"

"He can't understand about planets and comets," Walt objected. "They can't possibly study astronomy when the sky's covered all the time."

Greenie shook the design free and held his hands above his own head, like a diver. Then he parted them, slowly lowering his arms to each side, all the time staring up at the sky as he did so.

"Clouds? Clouds parting?" guessed Solveig, and Greenie nodded vigorously.

"So it *does* stop raining and the sun does come out?" Walt asked.

"And is it *then* that the wave comes?"

"Because of something out there?"

To each of their questions Greenie nodded excitedly. He put his hands back on their heads and Walt felt his brain almost explode with images. Stars. Wind. The sun beating down. Water shrinking back from the land and then coming in, a great wave of it. And between the drying up and the flood...something else. Something that Greenie couldn't describe in mere pictures. Something wonderful that was promised to all his kind.

"How many of you are there?" Walt asked, and Greenie's arms were flung wide, his fingers opening and closing to convey thousands of creatures like him, all over the planet.

"How come we didn't find you? If only we'd known in time..." Walt stopped. *Would* his father have stopped work if he'd known that Aqua was the home of the first known intelligent amphibian in the galaxy? He could almost hear the colonel's voice: "Stop terraforming on account of some low-life frog? You must be out of your mind!"

"Where *were* you?"

Hiding, it seemed. In caves. In the courses of underground rivers. Among the reed forests.

"But who warned you we were coming? You couldn't have seen the survey ships, not possibly."

But this question just brought another puzzling image, of a shimmering gold cloud that broke into individual units, like grains of reed pollen scattering and then coming together into a powerful something.

"Elders?" Solveig guessed. "Wise ones?"

Something like that. But more, it seemed. And that was all they could find out—that the "elders" had warned Greenie and his kind to hide from the incoming ships. And that the elders had something to do with the tidal wave.

"It's getting late." Walt suddenly noticed the darkening sky, the shadows deepening among the reeds. If they stayed out much longer it would be hard to follow the winding stream back to the compound. "We have to go. Greenie, will you come tomorrow?"

The amphibian made a gesture with his arm toward the sky. He knew, Walt realized, exactly where the sun was, even when it was hidden under dense clouds. He was pointing to the southwest. To where the sun would be at about four o'clock in the afternoon. Then he moved back among the reeds and was instantly out of sight. There was only the darkening marsh. There hadn't even been a splash.

They paddled back to the compound and stored the canoe. As they walked up to the cafeteria, Solveig broke the silence. "If Colonel Elliot succeeds in draining the marsh, will the wave be able to get over the levees? Everything's been changed."

Walt shook his head, glad she hadn't said "your father." It was bad enough anyway. He turned at the cafeteria steps to look over at the lights on the dinosaur diggers. They worked on into the night, still gouging great wounds into the marsh, deepening the channels, piling up mud and stone to make dikes. They had gone a long way in a few weeks, in spite of the snail invasion. This was his father's doing, and it was wrong. It was up to Walt to stop it. Only what could he possibly do?

He sat opposite Solveig, pushing the food around his plate. "Sorry, I'm just not hungry," he said at last, and left her sitting alone. He ran up the hill to the colonel's house. His father wasn't there. Walt roamed restlessly around the empty rooms, trying to sort out what he'd seen and heard and what he was going to do. It was hopeless. He'd better try to sleep on it. Maybe in the morning he'd have some brilliant solution.

As Walt started to get ready for bed, his eye was caught by the photograph on his desk, the one he'd brought from Earth. His father, the hero, with all the medals across his chest. When Walt had asked Aunt Gloria what they had been for, she had answered vaguely but admiringly, "For doing all sorts of brave deeds out in the galaxy, dear." And he'd been so proud, he thought he'd bust.

Now he wondered. The only deed he'd seen so far was the messy destruction of a million snails. Once upon a time, when he'd been just a kid, he'd dreamed of being as brave as the colonel, of earning as many medals. Now he lay in bed in the long emptiness of a sleepless night, and realized there was only one brave deed worth doing, and that was to stand up for the inhabitants of Aqua and stop his father from going ahead with the project. And he was absolutely sure he wasn't *that* brave.

Only, what would happen to Greenie and his race if he did nothing? He pounded his pillow and turned restlessly over, longing for sleep.

SIX

Getting through school on Wednesday was a nightmare, what with Greenie's face coming between Walt's eyes and his books. And then after school he and Solveig quarreled.

"It's all very well for you to say I should do something!" he shouted, after she'd goaded him for far too long. "You don't have the colonel as a father."

He glared at her, and she twitched her braid over her shoulder and chewed on the end of it, looking silently at Walt with her large hazel eyes.

"I'm sorry," she said at last. "I guess I forgot not everybody's as lucky as me. Mom's such a terrific person, it's hard for me to believe anyone could be that different. You really can't talk to him at all? Not even sort of sneaking up on the subject?"

Walt shook his head. He felt small and stupid and helpless, and this made him mad at himself and his father and now even at Solveig. He kicked at the porch railing. "I can tell you right off, he won't listen to me. And if he did he'd probably kill me."

She sighed. "You're exaggerating again. Okay, okay. Suppose we got some more evidence? Would you talk to him about Greenie and what's going to happen to Aqua then?"

"I don't know. Maybe. Yes, I guess so." He squirmed under her steady gaze, feeling like a wimp, and madder than ever at her for making him feel this way.

She ignored his mood. "So what we've got to do is get Greenie to tell us a lot more. Pin him down to details. It's all so vague right now."

Pin him down. Walt had a sudden flash of the two of them in biology class, dissecting the small frog. Pinning back its skin. He shuddered and swallowed. He really didn't want to meet Greenie again. He didn't want anything to do with any of it.

"Okay, Walt? We'd better get going before it gets dark." Solveig's chin stuck out and her face got that obstinate look that Walt was beginning to learn was no use arguing with, because arguing wasn't going to change the way she thought. "We'll grab a snack and I'll tell Mom that maybe we'll be a bit late, so it won't matter if we miss supper."

"But what about homework and—"

"Oh, Walt, don't be so feeble. I'll go by myself if you don't want to come."

So of course he had to agree, and soon they were paddling up the winding stream through the marsh to the place where they had last met Greenie. Walt dug his paddle down, turning it against the current so that the canoe stopped and its prow edged into the tangle of moss that lined the stream.

"Can you tell it's the right place?"

"Yes, Greenie's been here. Look." He pointed. Like a cobweb woven between the reeds was yet another twined pattern of fine grass cord. Intelligent life. Reading about alien beings was one thing. Meeting and communicating with them was something else. Part of him was wildly curious. Part of him just wished he were safely back home, canoeing on the comfortable familiarity of the Oldman River.

"I wish I knew what it meant," said Solveig, after they had waited for a while among the stillness of water and reeds. "I mean, we're going to feel pretty dumb sitting here if it says 'Gone fishing' or 'Come back next Tuesday.'"

Stay, said a voice inside Walt's head, and at the same moment Solveig said, "Oh, good, he's coming! Should we let him know where we are?"

"He already knows, doesn't he? And he'll have heard the noise of our paddles and the canoe moving through the water. Remember how sounds travel in a swimming pool?"

She shook her head.

"You mean you don't even have swimming pools on Kwatar?"

"Goodness, no. Such luxury!"

"So where did you learn to swim?"

"I can't swim. No one on Kwatar does."

"But you came out in the canoe the other day without saying a word. Weren't you scared?"

"If you must know, I was terrified." She blushed and laughed. "So now you know my horrible secret."

"You sure fooled me. Bossing me around like you owned the place."

"Sorry. Guess that's just me. The more scared I am, the bossier I get."

And you've certainly been bossy lately, Walt thought, with a kind of grudging admiration; but before he had time to put his thoughts into words, he was interrupted by a gargling sound. He looked over his shoulder and yelled in surprise, because staring at them were a dozen pairs of amber eyes. A dozen wide mouths. Identical, as if someone had hidden a triple mirror in among the reeds, a mirror that reflected Greenie's image over and over again. They were facing a whole gang of alien frogs.

Walt gulped and managed to suppress a second yell, wondering if Solveig had cried out too. It wouldn't be so bad if she had. If she had felt the shock of fear and revulsion that had swept over him. They were so *large*, so *green*, so *slimy*-looking. And so many of them!

To his horror the one closest to Solveig held out a hand and she unhesitatingly took it. "Look, Walt. They want us to make a circle, to link together."

She took Walt's hand in a firm warm clasp and he found his other taken by the frog creature closest to him. He drew back, but the fingers grasped his firmly—cool, damp, and almost boneless. He suppressed another shudder and told himself that it wasn't any worse than holding a frog or a toad. Then a voice began to speak briskly inside his head, and his fears were swept away.

"We are what you would call 'the Aquarians.' You can understand better now, can't you?"

"Yes. How…?"

"We realized that one of us communicating with you was not enough. That you needed a synergy—many of us working together—before you could understand our message. The message is this: You *must* leave our planet."

"We do understand that. We're sorry about the mess our machines have made. Honestly, we didn't know there was any intelligent life on Aqua," Solveig said.

"The others still don't," Walt interrupted. "And they'll never believe us. We're just kids."

"You must make them understand," the voice in Walt's head said unhelpfully. "We tried to discourage you by having our friends the snails dissolve all the plastic on your walkways and machines. But when you began to destroy them…" The words inside his head dissolved into feelings of overwhelming horror, disbelief, remorse.

"I'm…" Walt began to stammer an apology, but the voice went on. It was impossible to interrupt someone who was speaking inside your own head, he realized.

"So we withdrew the snails. They have suffered

enough in the defense of our home. Now we have to appeal directly to you. Tell the people who are attempting to destroy our planet who we are. Warn them that they must leave at once."

"They won't pay any attention. They..." Walt couldn't bring himself to say "my father," he felt so ashamed. Only later did he realize that they must have known all along, that they must have read it in his mind.

"You *must* persuade them. No..." The voices interrupted Walt's thoughts. "We will not show ourselves to them. Too many have violent and destructive emotions."

"They won't listen. They're determined to drain all the marshes and plant oil-bush."

The Aquarians looked at each other, blinked their amber eyes, and shook their heads. "You don't understand. We are not concerned primarily about ourselves or the future of our home. We are telling you that if you don't leave within six days *you* will all be destroyed."

"*Six days!* You wouldn't do that, would you? You're just threatening us." Walt looked into the clear amber eyes. They seemed to him to show only kindness and concern. "Anyway, you're just not strong enough. You don't know what kind of weapons my...they have. Laser guns, things like that. They'll destroy you, like they did the snails."

The heads moved from side to side in unison. "You still don't understand. We will do nothing. You are right. We have no power. It will be the..." Then came the idea that Walt and Solveig had been able to translate only as *elders*, though it didn't seem quite right. "The power of the elders. And then...the wave."

His head was filled with images of the clouds rolling back like a lid, of the fierce sun beating down upon the marshland, of steam rising in the heat. Then of the water draining from the swamps and suddenly gathering itself together in a gray wall to rage relentlessly across the face of the planet. Like a tidal wave. But not entirely. Not drawn by external forces such as another planet or an asteroid. Nor by internal forces such as earthquakes. This great wave, sweeping over the surface of Aqua, would be powered by the force of the "golden mist."

Walt shook his head. "It doesn't make sense. What's the golden mist? How can a mist be powerful enough to do anything like making a tidal wave? And where will you be all the time the sun's burning up the ground? When the tidal wave comes? Won't you be in danger too?"

His head reeled with the onslaught of laughter. Laughter and a blinding happiness. He saw a picture of hundreds of amphibian bodies withering up under the unaccustomed sun. Then, just when the horror of it was almost too much to bear, the picture changed. He saw the dried-up bodies cracking open, and out of each brown husk emerging a shining golden *something*.

"Like a butterfly," Walt gasped. "Just like I said, Solveig! Out of the chrysalis."

"Oh, Walt, look!"

In their minds' eye, the golden, gauzy-winged creatures rose in great clouds up into the sky, their energy crackling like summer lightning. Higher and higher they rose, following the path of the sun around Aqua. And in their path the water lifted too, following them, drawn by their power. They saw it gather in a tidal wave that rose, rushed twice around the planet, and then subsided. The waters of Aqua sank back to their accustomed level along the streams and in the marshes, leaving the hills dripping as new rivers ran off their surfaces down to the marsh.

Now Walt felt that he was back in the familiar cave—and he knew now that there were many more, that the planet was honeycombed with caves—and he saw the starry lights drop from the roof into the inky water and wriggle through the cracks of the rocks into the wet gray daylight, little tadpolelike creatures who would grow into amphibians like Greenie.

"And what about the next generation?" he heard Solveig ask.

"We will leave our children shining on the roofs of the caves before we shed our wings and depart."

Depart? "Do you mean you *die*?" Walt pictured them lying in drifts of dead gray wings, like summer mayflies under the street lights.

Their laughter in his head was so loud and joyous it made him dizzy. *Not like that* was the message that came through, but nothing more. It was as if his brain wasn't able to make any sense out of what was to happen next. It seemed almost as if they changed into a fourth-dimensional existence. He just couldn't understand.

The slender fingers that had been holding his right hand squeezed gently and released their pressure. He opened his eyes, which he had shut in an effort to understand, and saw that he and Solveig were alone. It was almost dark and, above the reeds, he could just see the light of the colonel's house near the top of the hill.

He picked up his paddle and backed the canoe away from the mossy islet. In silence he began to drive it back toward the compound.

"You'll *have* to tell him now, Walt." Solveig's voice sounded unusually shaky.

He shook his head and paddled steadily along the winding stream.

She couldn't see his movement from her position in the bow. "Walt, are you listening? You've *got* to, or we'll all be killed."

"No, Solveig, you don't understand." *She's bossing again,* he thought. *And that means she's as scared as I am. It's not just being afraid of Father,* he told himself. *It's only common sense.* "It's no *good* telling him." The words tumbled out as he explained, as much to himself as to Solveig. "Because he just won't listen. What we've got to do is tell your mother. You've said that she's understanding. That she listens to you. Okay, let's try her. If she believes us, she can advise us who to talk to next. We've got to get as many people as possible listening to us, believing in the Aquarians and their warning about the tidal wave, before Father finds out and tries to stop us. And he will. As soon as he hears what we've got to say, he'll stop us, Solveig." Behind Walt's eyes was the image of his father as he was in the photograph, square-jawed, tight-mouthed, his chest covered with medals earned on planets like Aqua.

Solveig sighed. "Okay, Walt. I guess you're right. We'll go home right now and tell her everything."

"Only we've got to make her promise..." He hesitated.

"Promise what?"

"Not to tell my...not to tell the colonel. Not till we absolutely have to."

Dr. Helgaard frowned. "What mischief are you two up to? You're putting me in an impossible position, you know. We're all employees of the Agency, and once we're on a new planet, the colonel is in charge. His is the only authority. To plot anything behind his back is—well—mutiny."

"Mom, look at me."

"Yes, dear. Oh, Solveig, do stop chewing your braid. It's a horrid habit."

"Yes, Mom. Only please listen. I've never done anything awful before, have I?"

"No."

"I've never broken the law."

"I should hope not!"

"Then trust me *now*. Please." She grabbed her mother's hands.

Dr. Helgaard looked at her gravely and then nodded. "All right. I promise to say nothing to Colonel Elliot. Now what's this all about?"

They began talking together, stopped and began in turn, interrupting each other now and then, each giving their impression of what Greenie and his brothers and sisters had been trying to tell them.

Solveig's mother listened open-mouthed until they had finished. Then she got to her feet and began to pace up and down the small living room. She ran a hand through her hair and whistled. "It seems so incredible that nobody on the survey team even suspected intelligent life!"

"Well, what were they looking for?"

"I don't know, dear. It's not really my field. Artifacts, I suppose. And signs of organized social structures."

"That's it, isn't it? They don't *have* houses. Even the caves are only used as a kind of nursery for the babies. They live in the marshes. Their telepathy must be what makes their social life work, I guess. How could the survey teams have measured that?"

"Hmm. Good answer. You've obviously been doing a lot of thinking about this yourselves." She stopped abruptly and looked down at them, her eyes sharp. "Now don't get mad at me. Just listen carefully to what I'm asking you. Is it at all possible that you've been hallucinating?"

"Mom! We're not nuts!"

"No, wait a bit, Solveig. It's a good point," Walt interrupted. "Only...how would a hallucination explain my being trapped in the cave and waking up outside?"

"Perhaps you found your way out and then forgot? If you were exhausted, dazed by your experience."

"With my rain gear neatly laid out beside me? There's no way I could have got back to the island, picked up my stuff, and swum back to the shore. And *then* got through the cave again. No way."

"And what about my hair ribbons untying themselves from the bushes and getting fastened into a cat's cradle inside the canoe? We both saw it, Mom, and I really don't see why we would have hallucinated anything as silly as *that*."

"That sounds pretty logical. I must admit that neither of you is behaving like a victim of hysteria. All right. I believe you. I just wish we had some physical evidence that might predict the onset of this supposed tidal wave. Something our climatologists could get their teeth into. You say it isn't caused by an asteroid or anything like that? Because if it was, we could get our astronomer on to it. But pure biological energy...oh, dear!"

"Doesn't our equipment measure every kind of energy, even if it's mental?"

"I doubt it, Solveig. Anyway, if I understand what you've told me, that won't show itself until *after* the metamorphosis of the Aquarians. And by then it'll be too late to evacuate the planet."

"How long would it take to get the whole work force back onto the ship?" Walt asked.

"Just personnel, taking nothing else? Four or five

shuttle trips, I'd guess. I'll make some discreet inquiries. How long did they tell you we've got?"

"Six days." Walt and Solveig spoke together.

"Not a lot of time. Look, kids, I appreciate the way you've thought out your plan, but I think we should change it a bit. Going around the work site talking to people at random isn't a great idea. Sooner or later it's going to get back to the colonel, probably sooner, and then you'll both be in bad trouble. Your father *is* the head of the Terraforming Agency on Aqua, Walt. We're all under his orders. If he says you're both mutineers, there's nothing anyone can do to help you. It'd take too long to appeal to the Federation for a ruling. What we need to do is get a critical mass of believers on our side before he finds out. Enough to force the issue."

Solveig looked at Walt, relief shining on her face. "You were right about Mom fixing things, Walt. I'll never doubt you again. So how do we go about it, Mom?"

"Try to behave as normally as possible during school hours. That'll be tough enough, I know. Then every evening I'll invite a different group of people up here, people I think can be trusted. Then I want you two to tell them your story just as convincingly as you've told it to me."

"What if they don't believe us?"

"I believed you, Walt, didn't I? I think it's the safest route to go. If we don't move carefully we'll all finish up in the brig on charges of mutiny, and that won't help anyone, will it?"

"What's a brig?"

"Oh, Walt! It means prison, army style."

"There isn't one on Aqua, is there?" he asked, practically.

"No." Dr. Helgaard smiled. Then she grew serious. "But I'm sure Colonel Elliot will think of something if he finds out what we're doing."

Walt's stomach gave an uncomfortable flip. She was right. And she knew his father even better than he did. He wasn't the only person who was scared of the colonel, he realized. Even the grown-ups were.

Solveig had started chewing her braid again. "It's a great scheme, Mom. But it'll take so *long*. We've only got six days!"

"I know. I'll do the best I can to speed things up. And one thing's certain, I'll make sure you kids are all off the planet before the sixth day, even if I have to do it at gunpoint! So don't worry about that."

"We wouldn't go without you, so there, Mom."

"No way!"

"Well, let's hope it won't come to that. Now off you go, Walt. It's getting late. I'll see you here tomorrow, right after supper."

He had hoped to sneak into the house unnoticed, without his father's eagle eye on him. But the colonel was in his favorite chair on the porch, can of beer in hand, feet up on the railing.

"Hold it, boy," he called out as Walt attempted to

slide unobtrusively by. "Where've you been all evening? Taking the Helgaard girl out, eh?"

"Yes, sir."

"Behaving yourself, I hope."

"Of course, sir."

"How's school? Are you settling in at last?"

"Yes, sir. I've just about caught up on the things we didn't study back home."

"Back home? Your home's with me now, you know."

"Yes, Father. Of course it is."

The colonel looked at him keenly and he felt the gray eyes boring into him like skewers. In panic he began to wonder if his father, too, could read minds. He tried to make his blank.

"They're not bothering you anymore, I see."

"Sir?"

"The other guys in your class."

"Oh, them." Walt realized that he'd hardly thought about Gordon since he and Solveig had discovered the Aquarians. "No. I was planning to learn judo, before my ribs got cracked. But I guess I won't need it. They're no problem anymore."

The colonel nodded a couple of times and took another swig from his can of beer. "Sit down, sit down, son. We haven't had enough time to talk, to get to know each other."

"No, sir." Walt perched on the porch railing.

"Judo's a good idea," his father went on. "Teach you to stand up for yourself. You know, you've grown since you've come out here. Filled out a bit."

"Have I, sir?"

"I think your mother would be proud of you too." The colonel's voice was suddenly soft.

Too. He'd said *too.* Meaning *as well.* Walt glowed in the warmth of his father's approval.

"As for Aqua," the colonel went on, and Walt jumped, almost slipping off the railing. For a minute he'd actually forgotten. "Everything's running smoothly at last. Within the next six months we'll be able to start planting oil-bush. Within a year they won't need me here anymore. You and I will be off to a new adventure, a new planet." The colonel's gray eyes, sometimes as cold as ice chips, shone with enthusiasm.

In spite of himself, Walt was caught up in the excitement. How lucky he was! How many kids had the chance to watch whole worlds being remade?

"It'll be good having you along," his father added gruffly.

Walt cleared his throat. "Thank you, Father. It'll be great." The words came out automatically, but, once they were out, he felt as if he'd just denied the Aquarians.

"I'd better go finish my homework," he muttered. "Good night, Father."

In his room he sat on the edge of his bed, his head in his hands. How could he turn his back on this father he was only beginning to discover? How could he scheme against him? It was so *sneaky.* If he explained really carefully the message the Aquarians had given him and Solveig, maybe his father would believe him. His hand was on the doorknob when his courage failed.

He undressed, got into bed, and lay, staring at the ceiling, picturing the worlds his father had conquered: Prometheus, Tallo, Ethos. And now Aqua. He could hear his words: "When your father puts his hand to terraforming a planet, that planet bends to his will. Nothing, absolutely *nothing*, gets in the way!

The next evening Walt and Solveig sat silently listening to the grown-ups arguing. It seemed to go on forever.

"Come on, Nora, be reasonable," the red-haired biologist called Samantha argued. "You're asking us to risk our professional careers on the off chance that these two kids are telling the truth?"

"If they *are* telling the truth, Samantha," a man with a beard interrupted, "we're risking our lives if we *don't* believe them."

"Is there any proof at all that these elders exist, Bill?" put in a third scientist. "As far as I can gather, you can't actually see them. They're just out there, floating around like—like ghosts."

"Energy anyway, rather than matter, it seems," Nora Helgaard interrupted, frowning at Solveig, who was looking crosser and crosser. "Perhaps inhabiting the upper air. Surely that kind of energy would be measurable?"

"If we knew what we were looking for, perhaps."

"Remember those magnetic anomalies when we first landed? And there *have* been intermittent fluctuations in readings since then. Nothing particularly significant, though. We put them down to some upper atmospheric discharge—like the Northern Lights back on Earth."

"We've seen nothing like that down here, Jacob."

"Of course not. The cloud cover would interfere with visual observation. But they might be able to see something from the ship. If there's anything to see, that is."

"Perhaps we should ask them."

"Not until we have to." Dr. Helgaard shook her head, and the man called Jacob agreed with her.

"Better to be discreet. The colonel keeps tabs on all transmissions to the ship."

"Right."

There was an uneasy lull in the argument, which seemed to Walt to have been going on all night. Dr. Helgaard appeared to agree. "I hope the children have convinced you, friends. They have me. If you do find any evidence, such as printouts of atmospheric disturbances, anything useful..." She hesitated. "I would suggest that you keep it in a secure place for now."

The adults exchanged glances. Samantha raised an eyebrow and Jacob whistled between his teeth, but nothing more was said and the party broke up. Once the door had closed on the last person, Solveig burst out, "Mom, did you mean that Colonel Elliot would actually destroy any evidence they might find about the Aquarians?"

"It's a possibility. We mustn't be naïve. This sort of questioning and unrest has happened on other planets. Colonel Elliot has a nose for it. We just have to be extra careful. You both did very well. I think you convinced them of the truth. Off you go, Walt. We'll see you tomorrow evening."

He left in a silent rage. His father might be a bit of a maniac at his job, but surely he'd never destroy evidence that a planet he was working on was inhabited by intelligent life. His father was straight clear through, Walt was sure of that. Headstrong, with a wicked temper. But straight. When he got home he almost told him, just to prove he was right. But at the last minute his nerve left him.

"Good night, Father."

"Good night, Walt."

Again, it was hard to get to sleep.

The next evening wasn't like the first. Dr. Helgaard had invited a very different group: designers, project engineers, people who had worked closely in the field with Colonel Elliot on many other planets. Walt could see why she'd waited and invited them only to the second meeting. If one of them didn't believe Solveig and him and blew the whistle...He found himself even more nervous as he told the story of Greenie and the other Aquarians.

"How well do you know your father, young man?" Jock McIntyre, the chief engineer, asked when he'd finished.

His question was so out of the blue that Walt stared, bewildered. "N-not very well, sir," he stammered at last.

"Do you think he's likely to give up on terraforming Aqua?"

"No sir, I don't. He told me once he never turned back once he'd put his hand to the plough."

"*That's* true enough." Another of the engineers, a big man from Kenya, gave a rough laugh. "Remember what happened on Ethos? The water table fell drastically when he was through, and the salt water penetrated right up the estuaries. It was a disaster!"

"But not in the colonel's time, M'Kossa. Two years after he'd left."

"That's his style, isn't it? And what about Prometheus? Remember Prometheus? Billed as the largest terraforming project in this quadrant when it was started. Six years after completion they had to close the whole planet down."

"What do you mean?" Walt asked. "That's not true!" Ethos...Prometheus...two of the planets his father had been proudest of conquering.

"Six years of sandstorms. An ecological disaster."

"Aren't you exaggerating a bit, M'Kossa? You've got to admit that, when he *can* pull it off, the colonel works miracles."

"Right, boss. And maybe I'm talking out of turn. But

he didn't have to flatten *every* mountain on Prometheus, did he? If he'd just left a couple of ranges it would've cut the wind flow. But he wouldn't listen."

One of the others laughed. "He doesn't listen once he gets mad."

"And he's mad at Aqua. Those snails made him mad. Too bad about the snails." Jock McIntyre shook his head.

"The Aquarians were just trying to persuade us to leave," Walt protested.

"Bad tactics. You can't bully the colonel, as anyone that knows him well will tell you. He's a driven man. Driven by a dream...and maybe a kind of promise."

"Promise?" Dr. Helgaard asked.

Jock looked at Walt and hesitated.

"You mean my mother dying on Saturnis Five? He said that humans shouldn't have to live that way, that he'd always beat the planet."

"There you are then. Anyway, the idea of these amphibians metamorphosing and the energy of their transformation causing a tidal wave, well, it sounds more like a science-fiction story or maybe a myth than something biologically possible." Jock shook his head.

Walt felt a wave of despair rush over him, and he was astonished to see Dr. Helgaard relax. It wasn't much. Just the way her hands unclasped and the lines around her mouth softened. "Whether the Aquarians' story of their life history is myth or fact is not as important as the fact that they do exist. Since you seem to agree that they do, then I submit that we have no right to be here."

M'Kossa chuckled. "Got you there, boss."

"All right, all right." Jock McIntyre threw up his hands. "I'll send a report to Terraform Headquarters, and I'm sure they'll agree we should stop work and leave the planet. That's one order even the colonel will have to obey."

"But we don't have that kind of time," Solveig burst out. "Only four days now, while everyone wastes time *talking*."

"Solveig, that's rude."

"It's all right, Nora. Listen, child. There's only a problem with time if the story of the flood is reality, not myth. I'm not suggesting that your friends are deliberately lying, but the whole story sounds more like a race memory of something that happened earlier in the planet's history, like the Flood on Earth."

"They weren't vague about it," Walt insisted. "They said six days. And that was the day before yesterday. And they weren't a bit worried about the damage we're doing to Aqua. They're only worried about *us*."

"It's a hopeless time line anyway. It took us more than four days to disembark."

"But that was with all our gear and equipment, Jock. What if we were to cut our losses and run?" Dr. Helgaard leaned forward, her hands pressed together. "We could get everyone off a lot quicker than that, surely."

"An emergency evacuation, you mean? Aye, we could get the personnel off in four shuttle loads. That would take no more than a few hours. But the colonel would never permit us to abandon his equipment. Never."

"We could remain in orbit until the deadline for the flood was past. See what happened. We'd only lose a few days' work."

"Aye. And all that rocket fuel expended on evacuating us up to the supply ship! No, you'll have to come up with some mighty strong evidence if you intend to persuade the colonel." Jock got to his feet. "I'm away to work. Good luck to you all."

The other engineers left shortly after McIntyre, and Dr. Helgaard made cocoa for Walt and Solveig. "Don't look so doleful, Walt. It went a lot better than I'd expected. Jock's a hard nut to crack."

"It's not that. I know they did believe us, sort of." Walt stopped and began again. "Dr. Helgaard, what really happened on those other planets?"

"Prometheus and Ethos?"

He nodded. "Were they ruined forever?"

"I'd heard they might recover, a long way down the line."

"But *he* did it? My father?"

"Look, Walt..."

"How many others?" he burst out. "He told me about dozens of planets he'd remade. He boasted..." He choked and swallowed.

"He's had great successes too, Walt. He wouldn't still be boss if he hadn't. He takes a lot of risks. That's what the men were talking about. I suppose that's part of what keeps him at the top."

Walt shook his head. Risks were one thing, but the risks the colonel took were with other planets and other people's lives. He only half listened to Dr. Helgaard telling them the good news, that the meteorologist they'd talked to the evening before had found enough upper-energy fluctuations to raise some queries. There wasn't time to submit the data to headquarters, but it might be enough evidence to persuade the work crews that something was wrong.

"And they'll be the toughest to convince. They're the ones who'll find it the hardest to get jobs if they disobey the colonel and strike. We'll be meeting the union leaders tomorrow. The third hurdle before the colonel, kids, so you'd better be plenty persuasive, both of you."

As Walt trudged up the hill, he hoped his father wouldn't be on the porch again. He couldn't talk to him. He *hated* him. He slipped quietly into the house and got ready for bed. The photograph of the colonel watched him grimly from the desk, the level eyes below the hard line of the eyebrows seeming to follow his movements around the room.

All those lies. All that boasting. The medals he'd envied all his life. Aunt Gloria's stories. He had hated talking to the scientists and engineers behind his father's back. He had felt mean, disloyal. But not any more, he told himself. Tomorrow he'd really tell those guys.

He carefully pried the photograph of his father from

its frame and replaced it with the snapshot of Aunt Gloria. Deliberately he tore the picture in two and dropped the pieces into the wastebasket.

He should feel better now. But he didn't. He got into bed in a fog of misery and lay staring at the ceiling. *Maybe it isn't true. Maybe they're all just jealous of Father. And he's still my father, even if he did all those things.*

After some wakeful hours he got out of bed, fished the pieces of the photograph out of the wastebasket, and pieced them together with invisible tape. The tear went right across the row of medals, but the colonel's face was untouched, staring impassively at Walt.

I wonder what you would have done here, Mom? Could you have persuaded him to stop? Walt touched the mended picture with his finger. *But if you hadn't gone and died, he probably wouldn't be like this anyway.*

SEVEN

On the third evening Dr. Helgaard had arranged for Walt and Solveig to meet the union leader, Tim Rees. It was a disaster from the beginning. He listened to their story with an expression of total disbelief on his face. When they stopped he got to his feet.

"If it wasn't you talking to me, Dr. Helgaard, I'd be off to Colonel Elliot this minute, so I would, reporting the lot of you. But you're fair with the men and you've never been a troublemaker till now, so I'll say nothing about it, so long as you stop this foolishness right now."

"Believe the children, Tim. It isn't foolishness, I'm convinced of it. There are definitely upper-air fluctuations. That could mean..."

The union boss shook his head. "My crews'll never buy it. Sorry, doctor, that's just the way it is."

Walt saw Dr. Helgaard square her shoulders and stick out her chin just the way Solveig did. "You owe me, Tim Rees."

"So that's how it's to be? You're remembering the epidemic on Riga Two, are you? Well, you saved my life then and most of my crew's, and I won't forget it. But you can't expect me to work a miracle. My people know better than to risk mutiny against the colonel, especially right now."

"Why now?"

"In case you haven't noticed, Dr. Helgaard, the colonel's walking an emotional tightrope." Tim Rees's voice was heavily sarcastic. "That plague of snails just about put him over the edge. The least thing would set him off, and as for asking the crews to strike, well, you can forget it!"

"Even if they know their lives are threatened?"

"By a tidal wave? On a planet as quiet as a millpond? You'll need much stronger proof there's danger before I dare take it any further."

Dr. Helgaard sighed. "Even with the report of energy readings in the upper atmosphere?"

"Come now, ma'am. We all know that every planet's got its own peculiarities. I'd have to see the water back off and come roaring in before I'd believe in your tidal wave."

"By then it'll be too late," Walt interrupted. "Everyone'll be drowned. Greenie warned us, honestly he did."

"Greenie!" Tim Rees rolled his eyes. "Talking frogs! You'd make us the laughingstock of the galaxy, boy."

"But it's true, sir, every word of it."

"If you're *that* sure of your facts, you'd better talk to the colonel yourself, young man. You're in a better position to make him listen than the rest of us, indeed to goodness you are. But if you do, son or not, I'll give you a bit of a warning: the colonel's got a real short fuse these days, like I said. Think twice about what you do or you might regret it."

Walt walked slowly up the hill with Tim Rees's Welsh voice echoing in his ears. The path was dark, but through the drizzle he could see, over to the north, the floodlights on the great earth-movers illuminating in harsh black and white the steady destruction of Aqua.

He bumped into his father in the living room and found himself blurting out, before caution could stop him, "I've got to talk to you, Father."

"Sure, son."

The colonel seemed to be in a good enough mood, Walt thought, remembering Tim Rees's warning. He was going to have to take the risk, anyhow.

"Come sit on the porch." Walt's father plucked a can of beer from the refrigerator and took his favorite seat, feet up on the railing. He ripped the top off the can and tilted his head back. "Ah, that's better! It's been a fierce day." He wiped his mouth. "All right, boy. What's so all-fired important?"

Walt stood with his back against the railing, looked at his father, took a deep breath, and told his story slowly and as clearly as he could, beginning with the looped string on the walkway that marked the place where the plastic was dissolving, and the glimpse of the amber-eyed face among the reeds, and going on to his adventure in the cave and his meetings with the Aquarians. Some inner warning made him leave out Solveig's part in the affair and the last three evenings' meetings at Dr. Helgaard's house.

"And the Aquarians say that the tidal wave's only three days away now," he finished.

"Is that it? Are you through?"

"Yes, sir."

"This is some kind of sick joke, eh? Who put you up to it?"

"No-no one, sir. I mean, it isn't a joke, honest."

The colonel drained the last of his beer and threw the can past Walt's face into the night. Walt swallowed. His hands tightened on the railing behind him.

"You driveling little swine! Who put you up to this? You're too dumb to think up a crazy story like this by yourself."

"Nobody, sir. It's true."

"It was one of the work crew, wasn't it? Just what I need! Those damn snails! Damage to the equipment. Water seeping back in. And now a troublemaker. Well, I can handle that. There's always at least one troublemaker in every gang. I just have to ferret him out and then I can get on with the job. So who is it?"

The colonel was on his feet and looming over him. Walt could smell his sweat and the beer on his breath.

"Come on, out with it. Who's in on the plot?"

"There *isn't* a plot, sir."

He'd barely got the words out when the colonel's hand smacked the side of his head, almost jolting him over the railing. He clutched the rail more tightly and shook his head. His ears buzzed from the blow.

"I'll ask you one more time. Who put you up to it?"

"No one, sir. I'm telling you the truth. There *is* an intelligent species on Aqua. I've seen them. Talked to them. They did warn me. We'll all be drowned if we don't leave in the next three days."

"Liar!"

Smack. His head jolted to the other side. He felt sick and lights danced dizzily behind his eyes. He tried to stand up straight, to outface his father. Into his mind flashed the memory of that strange dream he'd had at the space station, where the familiar adventure of him and the colonel standing shoulder to shoulder against the dangers of an alien world had turned into a bad dream. A nightmare in which the colonel had become the enemy.

"I didn't make it up, sir. I heard them. I saw..."

"If there's one thing I can't stand it's a sniveling liar. You're no son of mine!"

This time the blow caught him off balance. His grasp on the low railing slackened and he tipped backward off it, somersaulting into the mud of Aqua.

Vaguely, he heard a voice. "Walt. Son. I didn't mean..."

He got to his knees. There was a hand on his shoulder. He shook it off, struggled to his feet and staggered down the hill toward Solveig's home. He wouldn't stay in that man's house another night, he told himself, and spat blood into the mud from a cut on the inside of his cheek.

"I won't go back," he said thickly, as Dr. Helgaard dabbed antiseptic on his cut mouth. Solveig watched with wide horrified eyes, and he wished she'd go away. It was bad enough that Father had beaten him up, but having her pity him was a whole lot worse.

"He can stay here, Mom, can't he? Just for the next couple of days?"

Solveig's mother hesitated.

"Come on, Mom. Three days. After that it's not going to matter, is it?"

"You can certainly stay for tonight, anyway, Walt. We'll decide what's the best thing to do in the morning." Her face was worried. "You told him, didn't you? In spite of Tim's warning. Oh, Walt!" She shook her head despairingly.

"I had to. Mr. Rees didn't believe us. Talking to *him* was the last chance. I thought he might listen to me. Don't worry, Dr. Helgaard, I didn't bring you or Solveig into it. I just told him about Greenie and what he and the others had said."

"And a lot of good it did you!"

"You won't let Colonel Elliot take him back, will you, Mom? Not after...after *that*. Oh, Walt, it's my fault. I did keep nagging you to tell your father. I'm sorry. I was dead wrong."

"It's okay, Solveig." His voice came out dull and flat. It *didn't* matter anymore, he realized. It wasn't like thinking his father had beaten him. It was Colonel Elliot who had hit him. He didn't have a father. He'd never really had a father. That was what he had to get used to. It was as if his father had died on Saturnis Five with his mom. He squared his shoulders and looked at Solveig. "We've got to talk."

"Mom, is that all right? Can we talk alone?"

"All right." Dr. Helgaard washed her hands and dried them slowly, looking from one to the other. "Make up a bed in the living room for Walt, Solveig. Don't stay up too late. He needs his sleep. And—you won't do anything dumb, will you, dear?"

"Do you suppose she guessed I had a plan?" Walt whispered as the door swung shut behind her.

Solveig shrugged. "I wouldn't be surprised." She opened a closet and took out blankets and a pillow. "So, what *is* your plan? And what can I do to help?"

"I want to get into the Communications Room and send a message up to the ship. To warn them about the Aquarians and the tidal wave, and to say the whole unit will be evacuating the planet."

"They won't believe you, not in a hundred years. Anyway, how do you plan to get in? It's off limits, you know."

"I've got that figured out. Remember when he gave

me a pass so we could borrow the canoe anytime we wanted to? It's still in my pocket. I think I could alter it well enough to make it look like permission to get into Communications."

"And what about me? Where do I come in?"

"Nowhere. I don't want you getting into trouble, Solveig. It's okay for me. I just don't care anymore."

"Thanks a lot! Anyway, *you* couldn't talk to the ship, Walt. You don't know how to use the equipment. You *need* me." Her chin stuck out in the familiar obstinate way and a painful smile spread across his sore face. He nursed his cheek in his hand.

"Maybe you're right. But you've got to be careful. I don't want him to find out you're involved. He really is kind of crazy."

Solveig shook her head. "I'm all right. I think it's you he's mad at. You're his son and it's *you* telling him he's got to give up Aqua."

Walt thought about what she'd said. *Betrayal.* That was how he felt about the colonel. Maybe it cut both ways; maybe the colonel felt betrayed by him.

"Well, I hope you're right," he said at last. "First thing in the morning I'll forge the pass and we'll try to get into Communications."

"It seems awfully far-fetched and hopeless. Isn't there anything else we can try?"

He shook his head. "Not that I can think of. And only three days left." He looked up at the clock. "Less than that, really."

It was the second thought that crossed his mind when he woke up in the Helgaards' living room. The first was the memory of the colonel hitting him. For a minute he grieved, then he thought: *It isn't really important, is it? Because in two more days, if I can't do something about it, we'll all be drowned.*

That second thought brought him to his feet, clutching his blanket, blinking sleep out of his eyes. Only two days! Someone should have woken him up. Lucky it was a Sunday. No school.

"Solveig!"

She was right there, sitting by the window, staring at the rain and thoughtfully chewing the end of her braid. "I thought you'd never wake up. I washed your shirt and pants last night. Here they are."

"Thanks."

"And here's breakfast. I brought a tray up from the cafeteria."

"I'm not really hungry."

"You've got to eat. Mom said, 'Make sure he eats before you start anything.'"

"She doesn't know, does she?"

"No, but of course she guesses we'll try something."

"And yet she didn't forbid you to…?"

"Uh-uh. She understands just how important it is. She's worried to death herself, you know. She was thinking about going up to the colonel and tackling him personally."

"You didn't let her, did you?" Walt jumped to his feet with a jolt that rattled his sore teeth.

"I managed to persuade her not to. Not yet, anyway. You and me, we're not on the payroll, so I don't think a charge of mutiny would stick. Not that it really matters if being drowned is the alternative. Is your face as sore as it looks?"

"Probably. I haven't seen it today." He managed a painful smile. Besides his face hurting, his ears were buzzing continuously, and he was scared that maybe he was going deaf. Not that it would matter. Drowning would happen first.

"I brought you porridge, so you wouldn't have to chew."

After the first spoonfuls of space mush Walt felt better, but he still had the panicky sense that time was racing by, that sitting here eating was a waste, that he ought to be off doing something.

"What about paper?" he said with his mouth full. "I ought to have something official-looking for that pass."

"I'll see what Mom's got in surgery."

He compared the paper she brought him with the pass from his pocket. "Just about the same. That's lucky." He pushed the bowl of cereal out of the way and began to copy his father's writing, substituting the phrase "admission to the Communications Room" for "use of a canoe."

"That's really very good." Solveig leaned over his shoulder.

"I'll fold it a couple of times and shove it in my pocket. The crumples will hide any faults."

"Don't overdo it, though. You don't want it to look as though you rescued it from the garbage."

Now Walt itched to be off, but Solveig persuaded him to wait. It was almost lunchtime when they reached the communications hut on the flat ground not far from the shuttle launch site. Solveig's intuition was right. Lunchtime, and there was only one person on duty, a young man whom Solveig greeted by name and began to prattle to in a language Walt didn't even recognize. The forged note was barely glanced at.

"A bit of luck," Solveig whispered when they were alone in the Communications Room, leaving the young man relaxing with a coffee in the anteroom. "He's from Kwatar too. I hoped he'd be there, but with four of them on the roster, the odds were against it. Now, all we have to do is push this switch down and you're in contact with the ship. Are you ready? Do you know what you're going to say?"

He nodded and hoped they wouldn't be able to hear the thump of his heart over the mike. He swallowed and licked his lips. "This is Walter Elliot, speaking on behalf of my father, Colonel Angus Elliot." It was the first time he'd ever said the colonel's full name or made use of their relationship. And the last, he told himself.

"Acknowledged. Go ahead." The voice came faintly over the radio from the supply ship in orbit above their heads.

"Colonel Elliot wishes me to report that, contrary to the findings of the initial survey, there *is* intelligent life on Aqua. Moreover, because of adverse weather conditions, it will be necessary to evacuate the base personnel immediately."

"Adverse...? That's news to me," the distant voice crackled in his ears. "Looks as calm as a millpond up here."

Walt swallowed. "It won't be for long," he managed to say. "Be prepared to send evacuation shuttles in two days at the latest."

"Acknowledged."

He flipped the switch back up and wiped the sweat from his palms. "What do you think?"

"You sounded very official, but I don't know if it'll work. They're bound to check back with the colonel."

Walt looked at her helplessly. "I just can't think of anything more to do."

"I know. At least you've tried to put them in the picture." She squeezed his arm and they left the hut and climbed the hill back toward Dr. Helgaard's house. Solveig looked over her shoulder and waved at the man from Kwatar. "I hope he doesn't get into trouble."

"It'll be nothing compared with drowning," Walt said practically.

"Actually the only bit I can't believe is the clouds rolling back and the sun coming out. The *sun*!"

"Suppose we *are* both crazy and nothing's going to happen. Suppose I dreamed up the whole thing and there aren't any Aquarians."

"Of course there are. It wasn't just you. I was there, remember. I saw them too. Don't give way now, Walt."

"What about hallucinations, like your mother said when we first told her about the Aquarians? Whole crowds seeing something that isn't there at all?"

"But she believes us now, doesn't she, Walt? It isn't hysteria or hallucination or anything like that. We *did* see the cave. We *did* talk to Greenie and the others."

"Yeah. I know." He put his hands over his sore face. It seemed suddenly chilly out on the porch, with the rain dripping in a silver curtain from the eaves. Walt shivered and followed Solveig inside.

"Actually, if I were you, I'd be worrying more about your father's reaction. The ship's radio officer is bound to check back and then he'll know what you've done. I think it would be a good idea if you lay low for a bit. Only where? You can't hide here. Maybe you should go back to the cave. You could take food and water."

"I'd have to come back in two days anyway, whether the shuttle's here to take us off or not. And what about you? When he comes around looking for me and I'm not here? You could get into as much trouble as me."

Solveig shook her head and began to chew one of her braids. Walt caught sight of his face in the window glass, darkened by the rain outside. It was swollen and puffy, like a gopher with its cheek pouches full. He flushed and turned away. He didn't want her pity. That was worse than the colonel's fist. He made up his mind.

"I'm not going to hide, Solveig. I don't care what he

does. Colonel Elliot's not my father, not really. He's just the man in charge, and he's crazy. That's what I've got to deal with."

He felt old, so much older than the wimpy thirteen-year-old who'd left Earth five months before. It was hard to believe that he'd once been like that. *I'm not going to be afraid of him,* he told himself, and braced himself for their next inevitable meeting.

It came after supper, which Solveig smuggled up to her house so he wouldn't have to be seen in the cafeteria. Dr. Helgaard was tidying up her surgery, and he and Solveig were playing a complicated four-pack game of rummy, when the knock came. A thunderous knock.

In spite of himself Walt's stomach knotted as Solveig opened the door. He got slowly to his feet and faced his father. For a moment they stared at each other. Walt saw the colonel's face tighten and pale as he looked at his bruises. Then his face flushed.

"How *dare* you go behind my back and call the ship?" His eyes were narrowed and bloodshot, and Walt could see a vein throb in his neck.

"I'm sorry, Father, but I had to do it. You wouldn't believe me. I had to warn them. In two days this place will be under water."

"Under water! You're crazy. Talk like that's a danger to the community. I'm going to insist Dr. Helgaard confine you to sick bay until I can get you shipped back to Earth."

"Father, you've got to listen."

"No, *you* listen."

Walt couldn't help wincing as the colonel's fingers bit into his shoulders. He held himself straight and stared into those bloodshot, mad eyes, trying to break through to the sane person within. For a minute he thought he'd succeeded. The colonel loosened his grip on his shoulders. A hand went up and touched his swollen cheek.

Then, behind him, he heard Solveig calling for her mother. A door slammed.

"What's going on?" Dr. Helgaard asked quietly.

"I want this young man confined. His lies could set off the whole camp."

"They're not lies."

"You too, doctor? And how many others are in this conspiracy? There'll be a court-martial before all this is over."

"You've got to listen, sir," Solveig interrupted. "The Aquarians *are* intelligent beings. And they're warning us to leave. We'll all be drowned if we stay."

"In two days," Walt put in.

"In two days, boy, there won't be a frog, large or small, left alive on this side of Aqua. Then we'll see what comes of their so-called threats." The colonel's fingers bit into Walt's arm as he pulled him out onto the porch.

"Where are you taking him, sir?"

"Where he'll do no more harm, doctor. Obviously I can't trust *you*."

"But..."

"And I'll thank you not to interfere."

As Walt stumbled along in the dark beside his father, trying to keep up with his strides, he wondered frantically how far human telepathy would carry to the Aquarians. He sent an urgent message into the wet night. *Get away. Hide. Before it's too late.*

They were down by the boat shed now, and for a moment Walt wondered if he could possibly break away, grab one of the canoes, and lose himself among the reeds. But the colonel's grip didn't slacken until they reached the door of another hut. He was thrown in, stumbling over a crate inside the door and bruising his shins.

By the time he had picked himself up he was alone. The door was shut. But there were no locks on Aqua. He turned the handle and then threw himself against the door. It didn't budge. The exertion only made his face hurt worse and his head throb painfully. He looked around. He seemed to be in a storage unit stacked with crates. Close to the roof was a small window, little more than a ventilation slit, certainly far too small for him to wriggle through. It was too dark to see anything else, so he lay on the hard floor, his hands behind his head, waiting for the small slit to grow pale as night gave way to morning.

Less than two days now. It was like a nightmare. If only it were. If only he were really back in his own room at Aunt Gloria's house in Lethbridge on planet Earth, with the photograph on the dresser his only link with his father, the colonel. The man of whom he was prouder than anyone else in the galaxy. The man he had always dreamed of imitating.

He groaned and rolled over onto his stomach. Eventually he slept.

It was broad daylight when he woke, and he felt better. The swelling on his face had gone down considerably, and the buzzing in his ears had stopped. Now that the room was light he inspected it thoroughly. The door was immovable and there was no other way out. He looked in the crates, hoping for something like a crowbar that might help him escape. Most of them were empty and the rest contained only replacement parts for the earth-movers.

More for something to do than with any kind of plan in mind, he stacked three of the empty crates together and climbed them. As he balanced on the pile, his head touched the shed roof and he found he had a narrow view through the ventilation slit, looking north to where the earth-movers were working. They were a long way from the compound now and looked like toys at the end of the ditches they had dug. Apart from the distant operators, there was no one in sight.

He climbed down and grimly began to dismantle the equipment in one of the crates. There were no wrenches inside, and he had only his bare hands, but at the heart of one piece was a rod that just might make a useful crowbar.

He reckoned it was about noon by the time he got it

free. No one had been near him. He had had nothing to eat or drink since supper the previous night. In spite of the humidity his lips felt dry and his mouth gummy. He had broken his nails and grazed his knuckles as he fought with the obstinate rod. When it suddenly slid free, as smooth as butter, he could hardly believe it.

He tried the door again, shook the handle, and kicked at it. Nothing. He tried to get the tip of his new tool into the crack between door and frame. He leaned all his weight against it and heaved. Nothing happened.

Perhaps the doorknob...He levered the rod against it, sweating at the unaccustomed exertion. Or was it getting hotter outside? With a sudden crack the doorknob broke and spun into the room, while the rod skidded against the frame, throwing him off balance. He poked at the place where the knob had been and the other side of the assembly fell off outside. He now had a small circular spyhole, but the door was as secure as ever. He licked his sore hands and yelled through the hole, "Let me outta here!"

There was no reply. He yelled again, listened in vain for an acknowledgment, and sank to the ground, his head against the door. He had never felt so helpless in his life. Now and then, not really expecting anyone to hear him, he continued to yell.

It must have been the middle of the afternoon, and definitely getting warmer, when he heard Solveig's voice in answer to one of his yells. "Walt? Is that you? Where are you?"

"Here. Over here." He knelt against the door. "A storage place. Near the boathouse."

There was no answer.

"Solveig. Don't leave!"

He suddenly saw a flash of yellow rain gear through his spyhole. Then he heard her voice.

"The doorknob's fallen off." Her hazel eye appeared in the round hole. "Hi. Are you all right?"

"I will be, once you get me out of here. I can't budge the door. I've been trying for hours."

"No wonder. It's been lasered shut, Walt."

The colonel certainly plays for keeps, he thought wryly, leaning against the wall. *When is a door not a door?* The stupid riddle drifted into his mind. *When it's welded to the frame* was the new answer.

"It's going to take a laser to melt it open again." He heard her muffled voice. "I don't know where I can get hold of one, but I'll try."

"You'll never get anyone to help you. Not when they know the colonel shut me in here. It's hopeless. He's going to leave me here, and I'll drown."

"He can't. He's your *father*, Walt."

"But he doesn't believe in the wave. He won't—until it's too late."

"If the wave does come, I'll make one of the engineers get you out. But..."

He couldn't hear her anymore. He peered in panic through the hole, unable to see the yellow of her rain gear. "Are you still there, Solveig? Don't go away."

"It's okay, Walt. I've got an idea. I'll be back as soon as I can."

"But what...?"

"You'll see. I don't know if it'll work. Hang tough, Walt!"

"I don't have much choice, do I?" But she'd gone and he was talking to the wet grass and the marsh beyond.

He climbed his crate ladder and looked out again. The rain had almost stopped and mist was rising in tendrils from the surface of the water, gathering among the gold-tipped reeds. *Less than a day left.* Maybe Dr. Helgaard and the scientists would be able to make the colonel see reason. Maybe the union boss, Rees, would decide to talk to his men after all. Maybe it wasn't too late.

He climbed down again and paced his small prison until his legs trembled with fatigue and he stumbled against the pile of crates and had to sit down.

Solveig, where the heck are you?

He stripped off his shirt and mopped his wet face and chest. The humidity was killing and there was very little air circulating in the shed. He was surprised that he could still sweat, that there was any moisture left in his body. He licked his dry lips again and began to count off the seconds and minutes one by one, concentrating. One hundred and one. Two hundred and one...

"Walt, are you there?"

"Solveig?"

"Of course, silly. Look, I went to Greenie's place—"

"How did you get there?"

"Took a canoe, of course."

"By yourself?"

She chuckled. "At first it kept going around in circles, but I managed in the end. I think I've made Greenie understand what's going on and what's happened to you."

"How on earth did you do that?"

"I knew telepathy wouldn't be clear enough, so I drew pictures. Look, don't keep interrupting. Greenie gave me one of his twined patterns to fasten in front of the door."

"What's the use of *that*?" Walt felt horribly close to tears.

"I don't know. Trust him. You're to wait till it's dark and then try the door. Once you're free you're to come right up to the surgery. I'll be waiting for you."

"You've got to tell your mom what's happening. Remind her that tomorrow's *it*."

"Yes, of course. Don't worry."

"Aren't you scared?"

"Part of me is. But now Greenie knows. I think—though of course I don't really *know*—that they're organizing something."

Organizing? What could a bunch of four-fingered frogs possibly do against lasers and earth-movers? And Colonel Elliot?

"Walt, you do understand, don't you?"

"Sure." *But I don't believe it,* a dull voice said inside him. *It's hopeless. We're trapped on Aqua. The colonel will never let us go.*

"Remember, wait till it's dark. I'll leave my window open and the light on. Got to go now." Her cheerful voice stopped. He wanted desperately to call her back, to have her go on talking. Being alone as it got darker would be the worst. Imagining the wall of water rushing around the planet, gushing into his prison through the slit near the roof. By then it would be too late. Far too late.

He swallowed and let her go. Later he climbed up to his lookout again. It seemed to be late afternoon. He found himself looking at his watch, as he'd done automatically time and again since he'd been on Aqua. Not that it would really help, even if he had an Aqua-set timepiece, he told himself, to watch each second and minute tick by until nightfall came at last.

He deliberately made himself rest, lying on the plastic flooring, consciously relaxing his toes, his feet, his legs, all the way up his body. He stared up at the small gray slit under the roof. He blinked and his eyes closed.

When he opened them again the slit was no longer visible. He got to his feet, stumbled over the crates. *Honestly, they seem to move around the room by themselves,* he thought crossly. He felt his way to the door. He heard nothing. He felt the smooth door frame. Nothing had changed. Almost half-heartedly he nudged it with his shoulder—and felt something give.

He stepped back three paces and ran for it, making contact with hip and shoulder. The door sagged silently open and he fell through, landing on his hands and knees in the darkness outside. He felt something slimy under his fingers and a familiar stinging. *Greenie's snails!* he thought, and grinned, wiping his hands on the wet grass. They've done it again. Aqua's answer to late twenty-first–century technology.

He got to his feet and looked cautiously around. Far out beyond the compound the diggers roared, their lights reflecting back orange disks off the mist rising thickly from the marsh. He had never seen the mist so heavy. He was almost choking.

He looked up the hill at the compound. Nothing moved. In the houses on the hill there were no lights except in the surgery. But something was different. He looked around, sniffing the damp air, and realized—it wasn't raining, not even a drizzle. He looked up, but mist hid the night sky. His heart thumped. The changes to Aqua were already beginning.

Quickly he climbed the slope toward the surgery and the small pale oblong of light on the left that must be Solveig's room. His shirt was slung over his shoulder, but still he was hot and the humidity was stifling, like the steam room at the swimming pool back home.

I should never have let myself fall asleep, he reproached himself. *It must be after midnight.* Then, with a jolt that ran through his body like an electric shock, he remembered. *It begins today.*

EIGHT

He had just tapped on Solveig's window when, behind him, the sky suddenly turned white, throwing his shadow, intensely black, onto the side of the house. For a second Walt thought he'd gone blind. The ground shook and the air filled with noise.

"What is it? What's happening?" Solveig pushed up the window and dragged Walt inside.

"I dunno. It was like an explosion."

"You mean a bomb? Like a bomb?"

Before he could answer, the door was flung open and Dr. Helgaard appeared. "Solveig, are you all right? Walt, where in the world did you come from?"

"I was locked in one of the storage sheds. The Aquarians let me out."

"Mom, I'm scared. I think it's beginning."

Dr. Helgaard shook her head in confusion. "A tidal wave? There's no indication. It isn't even raining."

"It must be the first sign, mustn't it?" Solveig

crouched by the window, staring out. "Greenie said the elders would do something. Oh!" She pressed her hands over her ears.

Brighter than the sun, the flash outside lit the landscape for an instant in stark white and black. Two seconds later the crack and rumble hit them. This time it was followed not by darkness but by another explosion and a column of orange fire. Lights winked on all over the compound. Questioning voices rose.

"That bolt must have hit one of the earth-movers." Dr. Helgaard leaned over the sill. "I hope the men got safely away."

"They warned them, didn't they? I bet that's why the first stroke missed. The Aquarians don't *want* to hurt us. They just want us to go away. Oh, there it is again!" Another crash shook the building.

"No living entity would be powerful enough to cause that, Solveig. It's only a severe thunderstorm, coming after this unusual heat..."

Another column of fire and smoke shot up after the third strike. And another.

"They've hit three earth-movers out of the four, so far, Mom. That's not just ordinary lightning."

"You're being overimaginative, Solveig. Your Aquarians can't be responsible for all this. They have no technology. And after all, the earth-movers are the only large metal objects around. It's quite natural that—oh, my lord!"

Walt saw her face whiten and looked over her shoulder in time to see a line of white fire flicker across the marsh from the work site. It ran like a river of flame toward the compound. When it reached the perimeter it stopped, divided in two and circled the hill.

"And I suppose *that's* just marsh gas?" Solveig exploded.

Dr. Helgaard shook her head helplessly. "I've never seen anything like—"

"Mom, *do* something. Go talk to Tim Rees. He'll listen to you now."

"You're right. Of course. I'll go at once. Stay put, both of you. I mean it. We may get orders to start evacuation procedures at a moment's notice, and I want you where I can get at you. Promise?"

"Okay, Mom," Solveig agreed, but Walt said nothing. He wasn't about to be tied down by a promise.

It wasn't until she'd hurried out that he realized just how thirsty he was. He went into the bathroom and held his head under the cold tap and gulped cool water. "I was parched!"

"You must be starving too. I've made sandwiches."

"Thanks. I guess I am."

They sat on the porch watching the community come alive. Lights were coming on everywhere now, dimming the circle of fire that surrounded the compound. Orders were shouted. A fire unit turned its hoses onto the circling blaze. The water hissed and turned to steam. The flames licked up again, unaffected by the water.

"Look, it doesn't go out, but it's not burning anything either. It's not like fire at all."

"More like pure energy."

They caught scraps of conversation from people hurrying by. Two men lingered by the hospital porch for an instant.

"Time to leave."

"Yeah, they're saying there'll be a flood next."

"After this lot I'll believe anything."

"But who's going to tell the colonel?"

"Him, I guess. Earning his salary, I reckon!" The speaker pointed.

"Rather him than me."

Walt recognized the burly form of Tim Rees running up the hill—to face the colonel, of course.

He gulped the last of his sandwich and got to his feet. "I have to go, Solveig. To back up Mr. Rees."

"You can't. Mom said..."

"*I* didn't promise your mom anything. You stay. I'll be back." He dropped from the porch without heeding Solveig's protest, "But that's not fair," and hurried after Rees.

He caught up with him outside his father's house. Walt had to admit that the colonel had never looked more magnificent. He stood on the porch above Rees, legs astride, like a giant. He was no longer wearing mud-stained work sweats, but the uniform he'd arrived in, cotton tunic and shorts, knee-high socks and boots, medal ribbons layered across his chest, his cap brim a slash across his face, shadowing his eyes.

"Order your men back to work, Mr. Rees."

For an instant it seemed to Walt that Tim Rees hesitated, and he doubled his hands into fists until the nails bit into his palms. *Come on! Stand up to him.*

Then Rees shook his head. "Respectfully, sir, I will not. We've lost every earth-mover on the planet."

"They can be replaced."

"They will not be, sir. We know now that there's intelligent life on Aqua. There's no man or woman here who'll risk their work permit by continuing. It's over, Colonel Elliot. It's finished."

"It's not over till I tell you, dammit. I've never turned my back on a job in my life, Mr. Rees, and I refuse to start now."

"But, man, you can see with your own eyes they're hostile."

"Hostile? You and your crews were frightened off by a bit of an electric storm. By a little marsh gas." The colonel gave a dry laugh, but Walt could hear no real humor in it, only desperation.

"Then there's the tidal wave."

"What tidal wave, Mr. Rees? Show me any evidence of—"

"You should have told us, sir. We shouldn't have had to get the story from your son."

"My son! No son of mine. A congenital liar. You're a fool if you—"

Walt stepped out of the shadows. "That's not true, sir. I've never lied to you. Not once."

"How did you get out?" The vein in the colonel's neck throbbed. His face looked purple in the strange flickering light.

"What does he mean, get out?" Tim Rees stared from the colonel to Walt.

"He shut me in a storage shed and lasered the door shut. I'd have died there if the Aquarians hadn't sent the snails to melt the plastic. Or would you have let me out in time, sir? Would you have remembered?"

"Lasered it shut? I couldn't have. I wouldn't…" The colonel's voice faded. His hand went to his head.

Tim Rees stared from Walt's face to the colonel's. "You locked up your own son? Judas priest!"

The colonel threw off his momentary weakness. "I've said he's no son of mine. Get your crew back to work, Mr. Rees."

"We can't, sir. I've told you, the earth-movers are gone, melted down to scrap."

"The men can dig with spades, can't they? With their bare hands, come to that." The colonel's own hands worked, the way Walt had seen them before. They had reminded him, then, of the way a potter works with clay. Now they were more like the claws of a wild beast. Cornered. Out of control.

"You're insane!"

"How dare you, Mr. Rees! I'll have you shot for inciting mutiny, sir!"

"No, you will not, Colonel Elliot." Dr. Helgaard stepped forward to stand beside the labor boss. "In front of these witnesses I hereby declare you to be of temporarily unsound mind. I release you from your duties and, as chief medical officer, I appoint Mr. Rees to be in charge until such time as you have been examined by a medical tribunal."

"You don't dare!"

"It's already done. The signal has gone to the ship and been relayed to the Terraforming Agency. The conquest of Aqua is over, Colonel Elliot." Dr. Helgaard's voice was flat, exhausted. It was obvious to Walt that this final decision gave her no satisfaction.

"And I intend to order the emergency evacuation of all personnel immediately," Rees added.

To stay and watch the final disintegration of the colonel's authority was more than Walt could stand. He turned his back and ran down the hill to Solveig's house.

"It's all right. Your mother's fixed it. She and Tim Rees. It's over. We're leaving Aqua!"

Solveig jumped to her feet and hugged him. "We did it! We did it!"

He stood like a log, his arms limply at his sides, unable to hug her back.

Solveig seemed to understand. "Oh, Walt, I'm sorry. But the truth had to come out. It's not your fault."

"I know." He stared wretchedly ahead of him.

"Well, let's not waste time standing here. We can

make ourselves useful packing up Mom's surgery."

"I thought we couldn't take anything with us? Emergency evacuation, Tim Rees said."

"That means just what we can take in our pockets. No personal baggage. But I know Mom will want her notes and a few special instruments. I can save those for her. There's a bag in the closet over there." She turned at the surgery door. "What about you? Is there anything you want to save? From up at the house?"

Walt shook his head. There was only the torn portrait of the colonel and the snap of Aunt Gloria. He could take plenty more of her once he was home in Lethbridge.

By the time they were done, Dr. Helgaard was back. "Okay, kids, off you go. They're sending all you youngsters up on the first shuttle."

"What about my...about the colonel? Where is he?"

"I'm sorry, Walt. I don't know. I intended to put him into protective custody and get him safely aboard straight away, but unfortunately he broke away from the men who were escorting him. They're out looking for him now. Don't worry. The compound is small enough that he can't have got far."

"What if you don't find him?"

She returned his gaze steadily. "We won't wait, Walt. You better than anyone know that. We must get the last shuttle off the ground by noon."

Walt handed the bag they'd packed to Solveig. "I've got to go look for him."

"No, Walt. I forbid it."

"Sorry, Dr. Helgaard. You're not my mom. And it's something I just have to do."

She hesitated and then nodded. "All right. I'll warn the loading crew that you'll be on the last shuttle. Mind that you are. Don't be late. Remember, it'll have to leave promptly at noon."

Noon. He went out onto the surgery porch. It was still dark outside, but the darkness was broken by lines of bobbing lights as people began to leave their houses and stream down the hill toward the flats where the shuttle waited. The night was now as warm as midday back home. The mist swirled knee high, but through it he could see the ring of light flickering around the compound. It was like a cattle fence, closed except for the one gap, the path that led to the launch site. The message could hardly be more clear. *Go. Go Now.*

He peered helplessly around, confused by the moving flashlights and the patterns of light and shadow they threw against the sides of the buildings. Somewhere, hiding in the dark, was his father.

Walt decided to begin his search at the top of the hill, in the house he had never learned to call home, and then spiral his way down. The door was open. He pushed it cautiously wider and went in, bracing himself for a sudden violent encounter. But the living room was empty, as were both bedrooms and the bathroom. There was only the colonel's office left. It seemed as if a small intense storm had passed through. Torn papers lay everywhere, files were overturned. The colonel's rage was evident. But the colonel himself had gone. He thought of his mother's photograph, but there wasn't time to look.

Walt circled the outside of the house and then moved downhill, leaving the straight walkways to comb the shadowy areas between the houses. The ground was slick and walking wasn't easy, but he plodded doggedly on. At every house he knocked on the door and asked if they had seen the colonel. Where the occupants had already left, he searched the rooms quickly and moved on.

A column of fire and the sound of thunder over to the northwest stopped him for a minute. But this time it wasn't another warning from the Aquarian elders—just the first shuttle taking off for the ship. He watched its flight upward to safety. Three more to go. The sky was getting light over in the east, far lighter than a normal Aquarian dawn. It hadn't rained for almost twenty-four hours.

The sun rose huge and red through the low blanket of mist as he searched the cafeteria, the school, the labs. By the time the second shuttle had descended from the ship and then taken off again, he could no longer see its trail through the sky, the sun was so bright.

Two men jogged down the hill. "On your way, young man. Only two shuttles to go."

"I'm still looking for the colonel."

The first man laughed. "You'll never get him on a shuttle if he doesn't want to go. He's gone nuts, they say."

"Shut your mouth, stupid," the second hissed. "That's his son you're talking to."

Walt searched doggedly on. *His son.* He felt his lips move, and form the word *father.* He shouted it out loud and listened for an answer. The sun had burned the mist away and the reeds stood tall as sentinels in water that was as still as oil. He'd looked everywhere now except the storage sheds. The ground shook behind him as the third shuttle took off. The sun was blazing relentlessly down. He could feel his skin tighten and prickle with the heat. The air shimmered like Lethbridge in the grip of a heat wave.

Only the boat shed now. He tore open the door, bracing himself for the encounter. But nobody was there. As he turned back to the door his mind suddenly registered the fact that there were only *three* boats, where there should have been four. Should he take off in one of them and try to find his father? Was there time? In the split second of hesitation he saw the lasered holes in the hulls of the remaining canoes. The colonel had covered his retreat and made it clear that he would not be rescued.

There was nothing more Walt could do. He straightened up and felt a most unexpected sadness flood through his body, washing away the last vestiges of anger and resentment. His father was as good as dead. He was still staring at the canoes when he realized that it must be almost noon. Time for the last shuttle!

Walt began to run toward the launch site, his heart

pounding. The shuttle seemed to shimmer and shift in the hot air and, for a terrifying moment, he thought he was too late. He began to yell and wave his arms as he ran. The normally muddy surface of the site had baked clay-hard in the unusual heat, and he stumbled over a rocky rut, saved himself, and ran on.

He arrived, gasping, the sweat running down his face, a stitch knifing his side. He rubbed a hand over his eyes and looked around. It was all right. There were still a handful of people standing outside the shuttle, technicians, mariners. One, with a clipboard in hand, automatically ticked him off his list.

"That was a close thing. Another moment and we'd have—"

Another interrupted. "Hey, you're the colonel's son, aren't you? Any sign of...?"

He shook his head, his chest heaving.

"We ought to wait," he heard one of the mariners mutter.

"We've got our orders, man. Noon. It's noon now."

"It's going to look kind of weird in the inquiry. Everyone evacuated except the colonel. A new twist on *Mutiny on the Bounty*."

"Don't wait," Walt managed to gasp. "He's not coming."

"Is he dead then? Almighty!"

"Not yet. But he took one of the canoes out and disabled the rest. He doesn't *want* us to follow him." His throat closed up and he turned and stumbled blindly into the shuttle.

He was faintly aware of the final crash of the outer doors behind him. Of the whine of the airlock door closing. Then a kindly hand was on his shoulder, propelling him to a couch. He lay back and allowed them to strap him in. Then came the hammering rocket roar, the G-forces pushing his body back into the couch, blotting out everything except the sensation of driving upward toward the supply ship and safety.

The acceleration didn't last long. They docked with the supply ship and, miserably, he followed the others aboard. The kids were all crowded around the viewing screens, Gordon and the others among them. He veered away from them and looked around the packed room for Solveig. There she was, chewing one of her braids and staring intently down at Aqua. He stood quietly behind her, looking over her shoulder at the screen.

The ship had been parked in synchronous orbit ever since they had arrived on Aqua. As it matched the pace of Aqua's daily rotation on its axis, they had a direct view down onto the work area. Even from this height Walt could see the small dark scars where the earth-movers had torn into the surface of Aqua. Wounds caused by Colonel Elliot, planet maker. It was almost unbearable and he let out an involuntary groan. Solveig turned. Her face was grubby and stained with tears. "Oh, Walt, you're all right. I thought—"

"I made the last shuttle."

She made room for him beside her at the viewing screen. "And your father? The colonel?"

Walt shook his head. He couldn't say anything. She squeezed his arm and whispered, "I'm so sorry."

He squeezed back and then put his arm around her shoulder. Her body felt warm and comforting. He was glad she was there, but glad too that they weren't looking at each other. He blinked and stared at the screen.

A mariner, seeing the planet for the first time now, would never think of calling it Aqua. The daytime side was drying up and it was now more green and brown than blue. Somewhere down there the colonel was paddling. What would he do when the waters dried up beneath his canoe? Would he rage and swear, the vein in his throat throbbing with anger? Or would he wait patiently for the waters to rise once more? Would he try to outride the tidal wave? Had that been his intention rather than blind suicide? Was it possible? And if he did succeed, what then? When they sent a shuttle down for him, what would he do?

It was really stupid, but he found himself wishing he'd stopped long enough to pick up that photograph, torn in anger and mended—in love? The colonel had disowned him. "You're no son of mine," he'd said. But if it came to that, he, Walt, had disowned his father. But now that the colonel had been left behind, he felt as if this man had been a part of his own body. Not something absolutely vital, maybe something like a hand. Now that part had been torn away from him, and his whole body hurt. He told himself that the pain would go, that there would probably be a day when he wouldn't even remember this pain. But still it hurt.

If only his father hadn't let him down.

That's not fair, another part of him criticized. *It was you who made him into a kind of god, not the colonel. If you're disappointed, it's because your dream of him wasn't real. You can't blame him for that.*

"If only we'd been friends," he said aloud.

Solveig suddenly leaned forward and adjusted the focus of the viewing screen. Close up. A familiar view of the two hills and the marsh between—or what had been the marsh, now baked dry. "I thought I saw—"

"*Dad?* Where?"

"No, sorry. Not him. But look over there."

She pointed to the brown, dried-out marsh. He blinked and stared. A cloud of shimmering gold dust rose from the hard ground. It swirled, now coming together in drops like quicksilver, now scattering like motes in sunlight.

"Solveig, what...?"

"It's Greenie and his brothers and sisters. The new Aquarians!"

"Yes, of course." He stared in wonder, suddenly happy.

A voice behind him yelled, "Look over to the east," and Solveig quickly switched the focus of the screen to show the whole face of Aqua again. It too was changing. Like an eyelid slowly closing over its orb, a line of grayish white filmed across the brown land from east to west. Now it was directly beneath them. From this altitude it seemed to have no depth, to be no more than a film, a tissue-thin layer of water, but behind it the scars of the diggings had already washed away.

Now it was level with the top of the hill. It must have covered the colonel's house. The crest of the other hill had vanished also, and Walt could imagine the water pouring down the sinkhole into the dark lake below. The level of the lake rising to wash away the star-shining embryos that clung to the roof of the cave. Soon, like tadpoles, they would be following the underground currents, wriggling out into the streams to repopulate the marshes and rivers of Aqua. For some twenty years, if he and Solveig had understood their story, the tadpoles would grow into amphibians like Greenie. Then, at the end of that time, the elders would once more roll back the clouds and bring another tidal wave across their planet. Birth. Death. Renewal.

As they watched, the tidal wave passed. Slowly the tips of the two hills reappeared. Now the gold Aquarians moved in threads and knots, patterning the designs they had once made with grass fibers among the reeds. It was like a joyful dance, high in the air above the hill with the cave. Then they were drawn, like a single gold thread onto a spindle, down into the dark spot that was the sinkhole. There in the gentle darkness, Walt realized, would be born the next generation of Aquarians.

What would happen after that? According to Greenie, they would lose their wings and become something even greater. He guessed that they would join the elders, or whatever entity it was that had made the lightning bolts and the fires of the night before. Greenie would be part of something too great and magnificent for Walt to be able to think of him as a friend any more.

"Good-bye, Greenie," he whispered and felt Solveig's warm hand in his. She too must be remembering the amber eyes, the wide smile, the touch of a cool damp hand. Alien, but joined in mutual understanding and concern. So not really alien after all.

It was over at last. Aqua would heal, and the damage the colonel had caused would vanish as if it never had existed. But what about him? Would the Aquarians bury his body in some cave? There was certainly no way he could have survived the turmoil of that overwhelming wave.

"Good-bye, Dad," Walt whispered. He closed his eyes and tried to pray for the strong, willful, angry man who had been his father.

There was a sudden commotion. Shouts. The scream of the alarm klaxon. The sound of feet pounding on metal floors. His eyes flew open in time to catch a glimpse of a ball of energy on the screen, as bright as the sun, too bright to look at steadily. It rose directly from the marsh beneath them. Cigar-shaped, like a torpedo, it headed straight for the ship. Then all the viewing screens went blank.

NINE

"It's attacking the ship!"

"It's hit us near the aft shuttle bay."

"Hold on, everyone."

Clutching each other, they waited for the explosion, for the catastrophic instant when the hull would tear open, scattering them in helpless freefall over the surface of the planet—their punishment for the despoiling of Aqua. As the ship trembled under the impact, Walt just had time to think: *Greenie, you wouldn't!*

Then everything was normal once again. The viewing screens suddenly snapped on and everyone crowded close. It appeared that they were still in a safe orbit. Below them they could see the waters receding peacefully.

For just an instant it seemed to Walt that, out of the mist that swirled over the surface of the retreating waters, a face appeared, an outline as wide as the marsh. Amber-eyed. Grinning broadly. He turned to Solveig.

She chuckled. "Greenie, saying good-bye."

No one else seemed to have noticed. Perhaps it had been no more than an illusion, for now the clouds were beginning to roll in, blanketing the marsh, the hill, the secret cave. Down there, on the surface of Aqua, it was probably starting to rain again. And they were all still alive. All except...

"Walter Elliot? You're Walter Elliot?" A stranger in a mariner's uniform was tapping his shoulder. He turned, still dazed by what he had seen.

"Yes?"

"It's about your father. The captain wants to see you."

Numb and bewildered, Walt followed the man.

"It doesn't make any scientific sense," the captain told him, in a private and unofficial conversation in his cabin. "What our instruments measured, just before the screens went blank, was a concentration of extremely high energy coming straight for the ship. Naturally we thought we were being attacked by whatever force had destroyed the earth-movers last night. We attempted to defend ourselves, but our communications systems immediately blacked out. Every one of them, including our backup systems. For a full minute we were, to all intents and purposes, blind and deaf."

"But they never did want to harm us, did they?"

"No, that's true. But of course we still had to protect ourselves. How were we to know? Anyway, at the end of a minute we found ourselves back in control, though I have to admit it wasn't through anything *we* did. There was no sign of the energy blob. There was no damage to the hull. But our computer indicated that one of the shuttle bays had been opened and then closed again. I mean, from the *outside*." The captain laughed nervously. "You've got to understand that what I'm telling you couldn't possibly happen. It *couldn't* have happened. What I'm going to report in the ship's log I can't imagine, but it certainly won't be that."

"I don't understand, sir. What did happen?"

"We found that the air pumps in the aft shuttle bay started working. Nothing to do with us, we hadn't switched them on. Once the atmosphere in the shuttle bay balanced the ship's pressure we were able to open the inner doors." The captain stopped, and then went on rapidly, his eyes not meeting Walt's, his face expressionless. "The shuttle was in the bay, undamaged. But on the floor in front of it we found a standard plastic canoe. In the canoe was Colonel Elliot."

"My father!" Walt jumped to his feet. "Do you mean he's alive? But he couldn't have survived that, could he?"

"When we went into the bay he was sitting amidships, holding the paddle," the captain went on in the same flat voice. "Just as if he'd been snatched from the surface of Aqua and dumped on my ship! Think of the energy it must have taken to do that. To transport him without harm, in spite of the lack of oxygen, of pressure . . ." The captain shook his head disbelievingly.

"Is he all right, then?" Walt yelled again.

"All right? Well, yes, I suppose you could say so. In a manner of speaking. But it couldn't have happened. It's scientifically impossible."

"My father—what does he say happened?"

"The colonel? Oh, he has nothing useful to report. No." The captain paused and then seemed to make up his mind. "It didn't happen that way. I'm convinced that the colonel came aboard in the normal manner. The tallyman missed him, that's all. The rest was hallucination. There'll be nothing to report. Except for the tidal wave, of course. You were right about that, son. How did you know?"

Walt shook his head. "That's not important anymore. But my father..."

He's alive, Walt thought. Greenie had done it, of course. Greenie and the other elders. Aqua was free again and not a single human life had been lost.

The captain broke into a smile. "You must be very relieved that your father's safely aboard after all. I apologize for the confusion. I expect you'd like to see him right away." He put a friendly hand on Walt's shoulder.

Walt felt his insides knot up in the old familiar way. He tried to take a deep breath and felt the weight back on his chest. He could still feel his father's hand slapping his face, again and again. He could see the bloodshot eyes, the tight mouth, the vein throbbing in his throat.

He swallowed. "I don't know. I don't expect...does he want to see me, sir?"

"Of course he does. You're his son, boy. Now I must

warn you, you'll find him very much changed. Dr. Helgaard believes that, given time and rest, he'll...er...normalize. But don't be surprised at his...er...his manner. Don't rush him. Come along now. I'll show you the way."

The captain's hand on his back propelled Walt out of the room, down a corridor, and around a corner before he could even protest. And what was he to say, after all? That he was afraid to face his own father? He saw the sign over the door, SICK BAY, and managed to draw back.

The colonel will kill me, he wanted to say. I've ruined his work on Aqua. Maybe his whole professional life. Me, his own son, blowing the whistle on his project. He must hate my guts.

"It'll be just fine, son." The captain swung open the door and pushed him inside.

Dr. Helgaard was there. Other strange faces stared at him. Walt sucked in his gut and tried to stand tall, his chin out. *I won't let him know how much he used to scare me. And if he finds out what I feel about him, well, I don't care anymore.* He caught sight of his reflection in a glass-fronted cupboard and thought, with a shock, *I look like him.* The same narrowed eyes. The same tight mouth.

They had put his father in a small alcove in the sick bay. He had let them remove his uniform, which now hung beside the bed, medals striping the left shoulder and chest. He himself lay quietly, in hospital white, blankets to his armpits, his arms neatly disposed at his sides.

At first Walt didn't recognize him. This couldn't be Colonel Angus Elliot, maker and shaper of worlds. Where was the narrow determined gaze, the firm thin mouth? He looked more like a small anxious boy, like Walt had been. It was almost as if they had switched personalities.

Walt found himself blinking back tears. He held out his hand and interlaced fingers with the passive hand on the bed. "Hello, Dad," he found himself saying.

The stranger smiled. A nice smile, a bit tentative, shy, a "wanting to be friends" kind of smile.

"Hello. Did you say...?"

"I'm Walt, Dad. Your son."

"Hello, Walt. I'm glad to meet you."

"Me too, Dad. It...it's been a long while," he ventured. The puzzled expression vanished and the man on the bed smiled again. "Yes, it has, hasn't it? A lot of years, I dare say. I didn't even recognize you."

"Maybe we can get to know each other better," Walt said cautiously, and he saw Dr. Helgaard nod encouragingly.

"I'd like that, son. Where are we going, do you know?"

"Back to Earth, I guess." Walt looked at the captain standing at the foot of the bed. He nodded.

"I expect we'll go back to Lethbridge," Walt went on. "To Aunt Gloria's."

"*Gloria.*"

"Your sister. Remember?"

"Why, yes." He smiled. "Back to Gloria's, eh? With you?"

"Yes, sir."

"I'd like that. I'd like that very much."

"You mean you're going to forgive him?" Solveig's eyes snapped when Walt told her of his meeting with his father. "I can't believe it. Not after the way he treated you."

"That's over, Solveig. The bruises have gone. It's okay."

"But how can you ever trust him again, knowing the sort of person he is?"

"The Aquarians didn't punish him for it, did they? And they had a lot more to forgive than I have. It's like...well, I guess, the difference between justice and mercy. No contest, really."

"And you're really not afraid of him now?"

Walt shook his head. "He's a different person. He's forgotten everything. Your mother says it may come back someday. That it's a kind of amnesia a person gets after a huge shock. I guess the Aquarians could shield him physically from the lack of atmosphere and from the G-forces when they brought him aboard, but not from what it did to his mind."

"So it's all over." Solveig chewed the end of her braid. Walt reached over and twitched it out of her mouth.

"Where will you go next, Solveig?"

"Mom says she's had more than enough of working for the Agency. She's got a job back on Kwatar. We're going home."

"Like us. But I'll miss you."

"Me too. We were good partners. Though I never did get to teach you judo."

"Come to Earth someday. You can teach me then, and we'll go canoeing on a *real* river."

It was early summer back in Lethbridge, Alberta, Canada, on planet Earth, in the year 2093. The water in the Oldman River was exactly the right height, not too fast, nor so low that the canoe would catch on the sandbars. They'd been out since before dawn, just the two of them. Aunt Gloria had packed a stupendous lunch, and they'd brought their tackle just in case they felt like fishing, but mostly they'd just been drifting along, following the current.

The rising sun had picked up the colors of the eroded banks, all reds and purples. Then the colors bleached out, the sun grew hot, and the smell of sagebrush wafted across the cool water. They were quite alone on this stretch of the river. They came to a place where a sandbar cut off a quiet bay from the main current and, without having to consult each other, they turned the canoe inshore.

Angus Elliot leaned against the back support and laid his paddle across the thwarts. It dripped silver drops into the water. He looked over his shoulder to where Walt knelt in the stern. "My idea of heaven, son."

Walt took a deep breath of the sage-scented air. "Mine too." He thought of Solveig back on Kwatar, on her dust-dry planet, and he was thankful for Earth. It was so beautiful. Maybe one day she *would* visit, as she'd promised, and he'd show her everything, take her canoeing too. It would be good to see her again. He really missed her. But he had his father.

The sun caught a column of midges rising in the heat. They looked like flecks of gold, and he was suddenly reminded of Greenie and the golden Aquarians. It was a pity he couldn't share those memories with his father, but that would be dangerous. It might bring back a more cruel past. Father was happy in his own small world, living on his pension, puttering around the garden, painting the house for Aunt Gloria, picking up groceries.

As if he'd read his mind, his father frowned and looked down at his hands, which tightened suddenly around his paddle.

"Is anything wrong, Dad?"

"I don't know. I had an odd feeling. Like a memory struggling to get out. I felt it all along that last stretch of river. As if I were in another place, paddling another canoe. Alone. It was like a bad dream. But..." He stopped.

"Don't bother with it. Let it lie." Walt's heart thudded.

"Maybe I shouldn't, son. That great gap in my memory bothers me. All the time from when your dear mother died till we met on that supply ship. That's a lot of years to lose out of one's life. Yet…"

"What's up, Dad?"

"Maybe I'm afraid to know. There's something about that other me…anger, I think. I can't remember." He brushed away invisible cobwebs in front of his face. "That other man. The one I can't remember. He…Walt, did he ever…hurt you?"

Walt couldn't find the right words quickly enough, and his father jumped into the silence. "So there *was* something. I knew it. I get flashes sometimes, like remembering a nightmare. Walt, you mustn't lie to me."

Walt looked at the familiar figure in the plaid shirt, his hands circling the paddle. "I never did lie to you, Dad. Except once about a canoe. I won't now."

"Then tell me."

"Okay. We'll work it through together. So long as you promise me one thing."

"What's that, son?"

"Just not to forget that we *are* best friends. Okay?"